TEXAS RELOAD

TEXAS RELOAD

A Sequel

Richard M Beloin MD

Rev. date: 03/29/2021

To order additional copies of this book, contact:
Xlibris
844-714-8691
www.Xlibris.com
Orders@Xlibris.com
828522

CONTENTS

DEDICATION

I dedicate this book to my two sons, Dave and Dennis, who as teenagers reloaded more ammunition than I will ever want to know—and at my expense.

PREFACE

This western fiction is a sequel to TEXAS LOAD. Although it can be an independent self-standing story, I include a prologue which will cover the essential events that lead to this current book.

If you wish to know the characters' intricate details that led to this point, then I recommend you take the time to read the original story as it was intended to be presented. Either way, enjoy.

PROLOGUE

How we got here

Being raised, in the early 1880's, on a Texas ranch near Dallas should have been more than enough for any young man, but not for the adopted Sam Balinger. Sam showed an early propensity for mechanical things and not cattle. So at an early age he knew he needed to start working in the machining fields, but also realized that it would take a sizeable stake to open a business in metal works.

After two years' work in a gun/machine shop, Sam was exposed to hunting down outlaws which resulted in a huge bounty reward. After enlisting Sil, a classmate friend, the Duo decided to enter the bounty hunting trail. This was the same time that Sam had an enlightenment and, started looking at an old school tomboy in a different light. All their plans were abandoned, when the sheriff's brother offered the two guys an opportunity to be railroad marshals.

Now the Trio all had different goals. Wil needed to build a nest egg for early medical retirement, Sil wanted to buy a cattle ranch, and Sam wanted to buy a metal fabrication business—plus Amy, that tomboy now a special person, saw some safety with three lawmen backing each other.

Working to arrest outlaws proved to be as dangerous as being a local lawman or even a bounty hunter. Assigned to the Southern Pacific Railroad and stationed in Houston, the Trio started their assignments. The first assignment sounded like a simple security detail for train passengers, until an outlaw got up and shot a businessman in the shoulder as he yelled, "this is a robbery, put your money in the bag or I shoot this man in the head, and one of you will be next."

Sam was alone in this car, as his partners were in different cars. He had no choice, so he got up and boldly told the outlaw that he was under arrest—under the outlaw's laughter. Sam never saw the outlaw's buddy in his back, but when he got close to him, Sam drew his pistol, shot the man in his back by shooting over his left shoulder, and then shooting the outlaw facing him in the head—all done with accurate lightning speed. The man shot in the shoulder was the well-known Ira Winchester of no less than Winchester Arms of New Haven, Connecticut. It was years later that Ira finally settled with Sam who had never asked for a reward.

After collecting their weekly wages, the Trio continued with other capers. To their surprise, each time outlaws were arrested or killed, the railroad would get the horses and guns, whereas the Trio would get the petty cash and bounty rewards if any were posted. Their next assignment was to arrest lumber poachers who stole virgin lumber from the railroad. As usual, these career criminals all had huge bounties on their heads.

During this time, the Duo had made personal commitments as Amy acted as Sam's partner, financier, and significant other. She had befriended Hans Stutgard, and given a deposit/promise to buy Hans's metal machine shop which currently specialized in fabricating brass cartridges. Ironically, the buyer of their brass cartridges was Ira Winchester, who was Hans's old classmate and friend.

Meanwhile, the Trio's life's controlling event was when the railroad president's wife, Mona Pettibone, was kidnapped. Her husband, Octavius, was beside himself when he realized that the gang would likely kill her, even if the ransom was paid. That is when the Trio was called.

The rescue was made possible by an all-out gunfight between the Trio and Butcher Howell's gang. In compensation for this rescue, the Trio made $100,000 from a grateful Octavius Pettibone, plus several thousand dollars from bounty rewards and petty cash.

It was at that point that the Trio was surprisingly called out on the street by Howell's brother and his gang of professional gunfighters. It was a fight to the finish. The Trio did well to not only survive, but put down every outlaw. Wil had suffered a superficial arm wound, as Sam put down three of the five attackers. No one realized that Sam had been shot in the chest until he collapsed to the ground.

It was a possible fatal wound, except for a new and young aggressive surgeon, using modern supportive medical equipment and new surgical techniques. After chest surgery to repair the lung and a long recovery, it was Sam who made the decision to return home and hang up his guns. His two friends were in total agreement when Sam received a telegram that his father had been killed in an accident.

The Trio made their way back to Dallas for the funeral. Afterwards, Sam proposed to Amy. Sam admitted to having an epiphany while away from Amy as a railroad marshal. It was then that he reflected and accepted that lifelong friends could become lovers, soulmates, partners, and husband and wife.

The new Duo quickly moved in together, became intimate, and started making plans for their future. The first thing they planned was to sell the family ranch to Sil. Secondly, the Duo agreed to attend an applied college to prepare them for running a business. Third, and the most important, the Duo finalized the purchase of the Stutgard shop. During their departure, Hans would be left in charge of five machinists, who would continue to make brass cartridges; and use the income to purchase loading components to include, primers, powder, and lead bullets.

Before starting college in September, the Duo got married. It was the same time that Sam, pushed by Amy, found out who his biological father was. It was Elmer Whitacre, the foreman of the shop he had just purchased.

After the wedding and a memorable honeymoon in a luxury hotel in Dallas, they closed the house they'd recently purchased, and went off to the Houston College of Applied Sciences. On the train ride, Sam divulged his hidden secret of having designed a progressive loading press and his desire to convert part of the metal shop to a loading center as a second source of income next to brass cartridge fabrication.

*

The life of a married student away from home was the couple's real and pleasant beginning. They quickly adjusted to the daily routine of classes and shop time. Over weeks they changed their schedules to be more appropriate for their long-term goals. Sam spent more time in the brass fabrication shop as Amy structured her business courses to reflect more the marketing and advertising areas as well as more exposure to metallurgy, machine shop, and brass fabrication to coincide with their new shop in Dallas.

Meeting their neighbors in the couples' housing units led to a long-lasting friendship with Glen and Irene Holt. In no time, the two couples started learning to dance at their Saturday banquets. This became a routine Saturday night activity. Sunday's after church, speed shooting competition also became a routine activity for the Duo.

Responding to some vague warning, Sam gave Amy a derringer for self-defense. A few weeks later, Amy was attacked on campus by a deranged psychopathic rapist. Amy, tied up to a tree, managed to get her hand in her pocket to grab her derringer. She shot the pathetic predator in the scrotum and permanently cured him of his lecherous behavior.

Before Thanksgiving, the Duo visited the foundry in Houston and arranged with the master mechanical engineer, Lionel Lofton, to have his progressive press's frame fabricated in poured cast iron. Over several weeks, the Duo visited with Lionel every Saturday morning to inspect and approve the press's progress. Eventually, Lionel's machine shop fabricated the five accessory parts that finished the working prototype. It was now up to Sam to manufacture the other 65 parts to match the 15 frames that the foundry eventually produced.

The Thanksgiving holiday was a memorable time for the Duo. Their family all day gathering with Amy's parents and Elmer, Sam's biological father, was a bonding event for all. The next day, the Duo visited the shop. They took the opportunity to emphasize that brass fabrication should turn to building an inventory of 38 and 44 special cases which they would need to load smokeless ammo. Also, to keep up with demand, the Duo decided to buy a second 5-man brass cartridge fabricator and let Elmer and Hans man it with new workers. To make room for the new cartridge machine, everyone got together and selected a dozen metal machining tools they would need in the future, and stored the others.

Returning to college, Sam realized that even if he worked every night and all weekends, he would not have time to produce 65 accessory press parts. So he made the Holts an offer they could not refuse, and hired Glen to work with Sam in the shop, and Irene to start sewing press covers and work with Amy in preparing a mailout to Texas gun shops.

By Xmas, it was clear to Sam and Amy that they would graduate in May and avoid the summer schedule of review and practice without new instructions. It was also a revelation when the Holts announced they were changing their majors to brass fabrication, and were not planning to return to San Antonio to work in the family plant—for very personal marriage threatening reasons. It only took seconds for the Duo to hire the Holts. Amy later admitted that Irene had been her first and only lifetime girlfriend, and had worried how she could ever let her go to San Antonio.

Returning home for Xmas was another family-oriented holiday mixed with business. After the memorable sharing of Xmas presents, the Duo visited the shop for another business meeting. The Duo pleasantly surprised everyone when they announced that they would permanently return by May, that Amy's parents would become shop workers, and half of the shop would be occupied by ammo loaders. To facilitate this, Hans was given the task of building a component inventory of millions of primers, powder, and lead bullets before May. The bank account was beefed up and both brass machines were committed to building the brass cartridge inventory.

Returning to college, Sam and Glen were busy fabricating those 65 parts. Things were going well and approaching April when one night the campus police showed up on the Duo's door steps. Wendell Winthrop's wife, Victoria, had been kidnapped and the sheriff, along with Lionel Lofton who happened to be Victoria's brother, were requesting the Duo's assistance. After a complicated and painful convincing of a captured kidnapper, the Duo met up with the Holts. Glen and Irene insisted in helping their friends rescue Victoria even if it meant a gunfight.

After the expected gunfight, Victoria was rescued alive. Wendell was willing to pay for their service, but the Duo and Holts refused. Instead they sold the horses, guns, and collected the petty cash. Bounty rewards yielded thousands of dollars, and the Duo and Holts ended up each with $3,500 in their bank accounts.

May arrived, the 65 parts were done, and all finished 16 presses had been shipped to Hans as soon as one had been completed. Amy and Irene managed to send out 200, letters of introduction and order forms, to the major city gun shops in Texas. After a well-attended going away banquet for early graduates, they made the final trip back to Dallas while leaving the Holts in college till the September graduation.

*

Once in Dallas, the first thing Sam did was to place an ad in the local newspaper. He was advertising for general light duty humdrum work with benefits and a living wage. Within a week, he had over 60 applicants that came to the shop to apply. On the day interviews were conducted, the list of applicants had been pared down to 36 people by the Backers, the sheriff, and Hans—removing criminals, no-goods, and philanderers.

The Duo went thru a designed physical test and the detail list of employment requirement. The physical test eliminated 10 people because of a tremor or poor coordination. The presentation of job requirements pared it down to 16 good applicants which the Duo chose to train for the 12 presses—keeping a 4-man backup.

The next day with all the presses available, he started the training sessions. After two days, each new loader started making loaded ammo under the Duo's supervision. By the end of the week, each man and woman were loading 1,000 rounds per day.

As the loading section was being started, other activities were going on. Sam with Neil's help designed a powder scale and an automated priming system that had to be finished by Elmer as the man with the most experience. The next event was an unscheduled surprise, the Holts arrived by June instead of September stating they were ready to work. The Duo understood that continuing with undirected independent experience did not make staying a worthwhile expense.

Another surprise was when Amy's aunt arrived at her mom's house looking for work. She was immediately hired to help Ida on the processing table. At the same time, Neil and Ann married with a get together at Darcy's Diner and a generous gift from the Duo. Activities at the shop were interrupted as the Duo and the Holts had to help Sil and Wil fight off an all-out rustlers' attack, and end a range war.

The last event of the year was the business meeting and dinner held on New Year's Eve. As part of profit sharing, each worker got $200 or more (an $8,000 value), as well as long- and short-term disability protection, three personal paid days, medical insurance, three holidays off, as well as a paid weeks' vacation the week of July 4th.

That New Year's Eve night, Sam surprisingly brought Amy up to date when she asked him what his plans were for the coming 1902 year. To extend the surprise, he offered her his 10-point plan for the new year.

***

And now the story continues in TEXAS RELOAD.

CHAPTER 1

Managing Changes

As I said, I want us to double the size of our factory, and eventually start selling my progressive loading press to large city gun shops. In order to achieve this, I have prepared a 10-point plan, that I would now like to present to you." "Go on, can't wait to hear this?"

1. "Build a 40X175 ft. new wing starting at the present front door.
2. Part of that expansion is the 25X25 ft. loading and receiving area between A and B-Wing. The remainder of the 40 ft. width will be a waiting area next to the front door and adjoining the existing customer service counter.
3. Move brass fabrication and machining tools to the new B-Wing—brass fabrication on the

left and machining on the right, as you enter B-Wing.

4. A-Wing will now be designated as the loading center attached to the processing tables with existing multi-use rooms.

5. The loading center will expand to a maximum of 36 loaders, and to handle this massive production, we need to expand our market to New Mexico and Colorado. I prefer we start in Denver with an incredible population of 137,000 and work our way south thru Colorado Springs, Pueblo, and Trinidad (total tri-area population of 60,000). Then to New Mexico thru Las Vegas, Santa Fe, Raton, and Albuquerque (total quad-area of 25,00) on our way back to Dallas thru El Paso.

6. At the rear of B-Wing, other than the steel storage, will be the processing center for the distribution of my presses.

7. Set up a contract with the Houston foundry to produce 100 frames and more when needed.

8. The machining section will fabricate all the parts for the press and we'll be selling the useless machines in storage.

9. Build our own catalog and call it the RED BULLET-IN. It will include every item we'll

be selling. We'll need a photographer to prepare prints for the newspaper printing department to make catalog inserts of each tool. Along this line, we'll need to create an operator's manual for the press, scale, priming system, and the powder measure.

10. We need to expand our building insurance again, but we also need to get liability insurance for our loaded ammo, and our many tools in the catalog, especially the press—likely thru Lloyds of London.

"So Amy, what do you think?"

"An amazing but massive undertaking. I'm a bit anxious but knowing that we'll be doing this together, then I'm all in. So where do we start?" Sam went first. "Actually, I plan to immediately work on:

- See Bert Holiday re construction.
- Advertise for another round of loading workers, and machinists to make the press's accessory parts.
- Contact Wendell Winthrop regarding the possibility of hiring brass fabricators and

or machinists. Either as May or September grads.

- Talk to the Railroad Supervisor regards getting that 20% freight discount and free passes that Octavius Pettibone awarded us.

Then, I suspect I'll be busy interviewing and training the new loaders while watching and monitoring the B-Wing's construction. What about you Amy, where do you start?"

"Before I start, we need to settle two very crucial issues. I've been thinking for some time that we might need a purchasing and inventory agent to handle the business as we have it. Now we'll have four departments: loading ammo, brass fabrication, parts fabrication, and a processing center for the catalog business to gun shops. That means we need to fill this position ASAP." "I certainly agree, but who do we go after? This person has to be very knowledgeable about the entire business from one end to the other and even understand metallurgy. It's going to take a very dynamic and astute person to do this job. This person will be going twice a day to the telegraph office and handle a lot of valuable vouchers and bank drafts. Anyone in mind?"

"Yes, and to me, this is the most useful person in the shop." "I don't know for sure since we have so many useful essential workers." "Well, who is the person that has been pulled off her station 7 out of the last 10 workdays?" "Of course, Irene. But who will take over her position with the loaders?" "Not sure, we'll have a meeting tomorrow with Glen and Irene to see what they are willing to do."

"Now the second issue. Expanding our market to Colorado. There is no doubt that Denver, with its population of +-150,000 people means about 100-gun shops. It will be very difficult to get addresses on these out-of-state businesses, cost a large fee at the town clerk's office, and take a month or more to get our mailings out. We will be ready with new loaders sooner than you think and we need extra orders within the next weeks." "I know you're right, but I don't know how we can do it any faster."

"I do. We need a man in Denver who can walk in all those gun shops, show them our ammo, and demonstrate the new progressive press. I suspect that the salesman will end up with paid up ammo orders, and even end up with paid up presses on hold till we can fill the orders."

"Wow, we're 800 miles from Denver and where are we going to find someone to work weeks away from home?" "I agree it will take a man with an unusual situation, but if we don't advertise for such a person, we won't know. So when you place an ad for loaders, add one for a salesman willing to work in Denver for 10 days in a row then have five days off at home—using weekends off, that's two weeks of work, one week off, and three weekends off." "When you present it this way, maybe we'll find someone in town, and if not, we'll start looking out of town."

"And by the way, when I was making a bank deposit last week, I was told that Western Union was closing one of three telegraph offices in town, and opening a new one in the industrial park for only business activities. That will make it easier for our purchasing agent."

"Great, then other than collaring Irene tomorrow morning, I will also be investigating and negotiating with Lionel Lofton of the Houston Foundry, Lloyds of London, and find a professional photographer to take photos of our press and the many accessory tools in our catalog. If Irene is not interested, then we'll start advertising for such a person in town."

*

The next morning, after the loaders got their morning tip of the day, they started loading as the Holts were called to the office. After Sam went over their plans for the year, the Holts were totally amazed and pleased to be onboard such a quickly advancing business. It was Amy who then took over. "So the reason you are here is to help us deal with the rapidly growing need for management. You can imagine the complexity in keeping four departments supplied with materials, and even become a director of press and accessory sales to gun shops. What it comes down to is that we need a purchasing/inventory/sales director. The one person who has worked every department in the past six months is you Irene. Would you be willing to become our most important person to keep this business rolling smoothly?"

The Holts were looking at each other as Glen spoke, "do you remember when we told our friends that we were changing our majors and asked if they would hire us; we had made a promise to each other. Time to fess up." "Well it's very basic, we promised ourselves that we would always do the jobs where you needed us. Yes, of course, I'd be honored to become your purchasing agent." "Wow, that's one hell of a weight off my shoulders."

"Now Glen, do you think you can manage our present loading staff by yourself, and the expanded one, once the new loaders start work. I will stay with you till they are independently loading, but then when the new wing is ready, I'm not sure we can leave you in the loading department. You are too well trained to not be used in brass fabrication or machining parts. Time will tell, but you should start looking for your replacement and even consider one with an assistant to replace you." "Will do, and I'll move anytime you deem it best for the business." Amy then took over and said she would spend the time with Irene to go over her new duties. "In a few days, we'll have our first foremen's meeting, and we'll need to have you present at all such meetings—as a forewoman."

With Glen heading back to the loading department, and Sam on his way to town to run his errands, Amy asked Irene, "this lateral change of jobs comes with a higher income." "Oh no, that can't be. There is no way a wife can earn more money than her husband especially when both are working in the same building. Our personal life is to want for, and I will never risk that over money. Actually, I'm willing to take a lower income." "I see your point, and I agree, but your income will stay the same as you will maintain your forewoman's status—which will give you attendance at the weekly planning foremen's meetings."

"So, let's go over your list of duties:

1. Maintain an inventory of loading components. Always keep a half million units of powder, primers, bullets, and casings on supply. It's up to you to decide when to ship surplus casings to Winchester.
2. Maintain brass buds—half million of 38s and 44s.
3. Learn the metals Neil will need, settle on the amount he wants for inventory, and maintain the steel shelves as such. For example. Say he wants five 6-inch plate steel, alloy #1189, and in six-foot lengths kept ahead. Then you order on your own once the supply gets close to five pieces. If Neil wants to change the inventory, he needs to let you know.
4. Maintain all box supplies: ammo, fixed rate 50, casings case boxes, press shipping boxes, and the many boxes for accessory tools.
5. Visit the telegraph office twice a day, 10AM and 3PM. Pick up mail daily at 3PM or send Cyrus if busy.

6. Pickup local supplies from Asa, the hardware store, the office store and whatever else is needed.

7. Keep 75 press frames on hand and order 100 at a time.

8. Process press orders as they come in, pack the presses in designated reinforced cardboard boxes. Same for the accessory tools.

9. Pay for all orders with a bank draft at the telegraph office. We will be adding you to the bank account. Sam will make all your bank deposits.

10. Always use Cyrus as your driver and protector. He'll be here every day at 9:45AM and 2:45PM to pick you up with his shotgun. Use a large reticule and bring your Colt in 38 special. Even if only in the industrial park telegraph office.

11. Don't be surprised if more is added to your duties as the business grows. I suspect the press and accessory sales will keep you the busiest."

"If ever you have free time, your help on the processing tables will be appreciated. Here is a list of the present alloys that Neil needs to fabricate press parts. You'll need to ask him the number of each to keep ahead.

Handle—Steel/Aluminum, Alloy #4129 in 3/16-inch plate

Ram—Steel/chrome, Alloy #6147 in 15/8-inch rod

Platform—Copper/Aluminum, Alloy #4744 in 2-inchX6-inch plates

Shellplate—2% Steel, Alloy #1909 in 3/8 inch by 6-inch plates

Toolhead—Copper/Aluminum, Alloy #5279 in ¾ inch by 6-inch billets

Scale and Priming system—Alloys 6266, 5910, 2164, 1873, and 1110

Powder Measure—sparkless Aluminum/nickel, Alloy #8229 and #8228 in 3/8 one-inch strips and ¼ inch by 3-inch plates

Receiving funnel—sparkless Brass alloy #1020 in pipe form

Belling insert—sparkless Copper/nickel, Alloy #3392 in pipe form

"I am sure the list will change and grow, but this is where you start. Sam is going to the bank as we speak and will add you to the account. See me if I can help you get started and we'll see you at the foremen's meeting this Friday. I will now inform Elmer and Neil of your position so you can start asking them questions if necessary. Good luck!"

*

Sam was the first customer at the Holiday Construction Company. "Hello Bert, I have a small project." "And that is?" "I want to add a second 6,000 sq. ft. wing to my shop!" "Whoa, tell me more." "Well as you enter the front door, the wing on the left is the present A-Wing, so add a duplicate wing to the right of 40 ft. wide and 175 ft. long. The first 25 feet will be the new loading area, the remainder of the 40 feet will be a waiting area next to A-Wing's customer service window. With a large archway, you then enter B-Wing. This new wing will house the brass fabrication on the left and the machine shop on the right."

"Ok, well let's go into specifics. I'll mention a part of the building and you tell me what you want. If you don't have a preference, I'll give you my suggestion:

- Floor—smooth concrete.
- Outside walls—same red brick, 10-feet high.

- Windows—all around but 6 feet off the floor like A-Wing.
- Inside walls—the new finished plywood.
- Ceilings—plywood painted flat white.
- Plumbing—none, instead add a water fountain outside the lunchroom and a sink and gas stove in the lunchroom.
- Electrical wiring. Your choice. According to code, we cannot place these wires inside your walls, these are two phase wires that can get pretty hot. They need to be outside the walls where they can be seen. Also by code, they have to be 6 feet off the floor with a branch going to a 3-foot-high surface outlet for each motor.
- Lights—every fifteen feet on ceiling. Four rows—2 over the machining tools, and 2 over the brass fabrication.
- Storage—only at the far end. A small power/furnace room, a medium metal storage room with steel racks, and a large 'sales' room with plenty of shelves spaced 24 inch apart for holding the tall presses. Plus a work bench 8 feet long with 8-inch shelves a foot apart.
- Heat—kerosene fired central hot air.
- Second floor—no.

- Roof and supports. Steel roof with trusses. Truss supports, two rows 15 feet out, with a clear 10-foot center aisle.
- Insulation—you choose. ¾ inch fiber board with moisture barrier on the brick and 9-inch loose wool in ceiling.

"Well that starts us off. We'll start today. The plumber has a gasoline fired ditch digger. He'll dig a 24-inch-wide ditch. We'll start with an 18-inch footing one foot deep, followed by a 2-foot-high and 10-inch-wide concrete wall before the first brick layers. The brick wall will be the slowest part of the construction, but with 6 brick layers and their prep teams, we'll have the four walls up in 12 days."

"Any idea on how long to open the new wing?" "Tentative 3 weeks, guaranteed 4 weeks from today." "How much?" "Commercial building in the industrial park starts at $1 per square foot and up." "Fine, here is a deposit of $6,500 to get started. I'm sure we'll make changes as you are building." "Great, see you in one hour."

Sam's next stop was the local gazette where he placed his three ads, for humdrum loading workers, machinists, and a salesman for the Denver area. Moving along, he headed to the Southern Pacific yard.

Addressing the yard supervisor, "Mister Wallace, some time ago Octavius Pettibone awarded me four lifetime passes and a lifetime 20% reduction in freight charges. I am now applying for these benefits on behalf of my company, me and my wife Amy, and my two friends, Glen and Irene Holt." "Well, this is highly unusual and will need to check with President Pettibone's office before I authorize these requests—that's worth a lot of money, Sir."

His last stop was to the telegraph office where he sent a telegram to Wendell Winthrop c/o The Houston Applied Science College.

Expanding business and need workers STOP

Looking for May graduates in brass fabrication and machine shop STOP

Will pay moving expenses for accepted candidates STOP

Offering a living wage, benefits, and great work site STOP

Will provide extra training to fit our business needs STOP

*

Over the next week, Sam was making a trip to the telegraph office every day after making his daily deposits at the Wells Fargo Bank. It was one day when Sam wasn't so preoccupied that he noticed a bank scene that bothered him. The bank door was left open for fresh air, the vault door was open. Several cashiers were at coffee break with their money drawers left open, and a gun toting scruffy individual was being served. Sam made his deposit and then stopped by President Cunningham's office. "Grover, this bank has poor security, why is the vault open and only one cashier at work. Hell, anyone with a hammer could rob you blind today, and the cashier that was knocked out would only know of the unrestrained robbery. You need to add some security, and lock that vault, or add an armed guard when the door is open. That scruffy man ahead of me, who wanted his $20 bill broken down, could have been a scout for a gang of professional outlaws." "Well, we've never been robbed, and I suspect we are naturally secure being across the sheriff's office. But I will discuss this with our parent company in Houston, since they presently guarantee us a 15% replacement if robbed." "That's nice and all, but how much do you keep in the vault?" "50,000 at all times."

"That's insane, and I have to consider moving my account to a more secure bank. I am not happy, and will let you know my plans, after checking your competitors' security."

The advertisement replies were coming in. There were 12 applicants for the loading position, one machinist, and one man applying for the Colorado salesman's job. Sam decided to interview the machinist applicant first. As the applicant walked in the shop, Elmer's jaw dropped, stepped forward, and said, "nice to see you again, Titus. Sam, this is Titus Harper, the best machinist I ever worked with." Sam said "Hello, why are you applying for this job, I doubt you're unemployed." "Well Sir, I'm 40 years old with a wife and three kids under age 10. I'm at the peak of my career making $6 a day without a single security benefit. I offered to take a cut in pay for just basic medical insurance, but I was told to look for another job."

"I see. So you know we provide medical, short- and long-term disability, personal days, paid holidays, a paid vacation and soon we'll add a life insurance benefit." "Yes Sir, and I'm willing to drop my pay to the current minimum wage to get those benefits. If I can't make ends meet, I'll find a weekend job. But I'll always give you 110% of my effort." "Are you willing to work under Neil Smith, the shop foreman." "Is that the machinist out of Whitehouse's gun shop?" "Yes." "Heck yes, Neil is a good man." "When can you start?" "Tomorrow morning."

"You're hired, and your wage will be $5 a day like all the workers get in this shop. Here is $100, a sign-on bonus, to help pay up credit bills and an outfit upgrade if needed. Now let me show you around and introduce you to my wife, my foremen, my parents/in-laws, and the machinists.

The next interview was for the salesman's job to Colorado. "Hello, my name is Ike Webb on Winter Street." "Why is that name and your face so familiar." "I lived in Waco then, and our team came to Dallas to compete in speed shooting. You beat me shooting, but then you gave me your speed-loaders as a consolation prize." "Yes, I do recall the day." "Well, as a Colt salesman, I requested being assigned to the Dallas area, as my wife, who is of poor vision, is now secure with two of her spinster sisters next door. I am gone for two or more weeks at a time. My pay is by commission for what I sell. I'm a good salesman and can average $4 a day with paid room and board, but not a single benefit. At age 50, my wife needs security and support if something happens to me, and that's why I am here. I won't deny it, I want security for my wife."

"Ok, fair enough. Let me tell you what we need. It is 800 miles to Denver, and we would put you up in a hotel with meals for two weeks in a row. We will also pay your train tickets, up to a two-way ticket every two weeks. You would work Monday-Friday. Saturday and Sunday are too busy in gun shops to entertain salesmen. We would pay you $5 a day like all our basic workers—or $50 every two weeks. In case you ever can schedule a visit to a gun shop on weekends, we'll pay you $7.50 like all other workers who work for time and a half on weekends. Choose those weekend visits carefully, for we don't want the word to go around that Ike Webb is a pushy pain in the butt."

"Fair enough, and with all those benefits in this introductory bulletin?" "Yes, all of them." "Great, so what am I selling?" "Two things, loaded smokeless ammo in four choices, 38 sp. light target, 38 sp. hot loads, 44 sp. light target, and 44 sp. hot loads. For.............and the case minimums. The second item is this press." As Sam points to the press on his desk. "Ah yes, I've heard about this thing and the many accessories that go with it."

"We'll train you to load ammo, so you can properly demo it to shop owners. You'll be carrying one in a molded traveling wood box with the loading components. You will be promoting this as a progressive reloading press for only Black Powder—without the smokeless powder measure and scale you will see in this shop. If you sell ammo, you take payment in a bank draft. If a gun shop owner wants to pre-order a press, he needs to pay for it and he will be the early recipient once we start making them. All money will be deposited in a Wells Fargo bank, and you send your deposits by bank wire transfer every week. We will start your own bank account in the Wells Fargo local bank and deposit your wages every two weeks so your wife can have access to the funds."

"After the 100-gun shops in Denver, where do I go." "South into Colorado Springs, Pueblo, and Trinidad where there are another 40-gun shops. Afterwards, we might go to New Mexico or who knows."

"So, what do you think now?" "I'm all in and I'm sure my wife would be ecstatic. I hope you are willing to try me out." "I am, you're hired. Here is a signing on bonus of $100 to pay old credit bills, an outfit upgrade or whatever you need. Come back tomorrow and someone will train you to become a loader since you have to master this tool to sell it."

"Oh, I forgot, every contact gets a RED BULLET-IN and all the accessories will be available for sale except the scale/powder measure—which are future items and you do not even accept a pre-order payment for these tools. The last points are that you promote this as a 'reloader' to use spent casings. Using Black Powder will not compete with our new casings and smokeless powder. The second point is that you are selling 'one' per gun shop, and emphasize it is for the gun shop to use to reload ammo for sale. This is not a press for the gun shop to sell to the public."

*

Days later, the first Friday's foremen's meeting was called at 9AM. As everyone was milling about, Sam noticed some crucial workers were busy talking about something interesting. Sam was going to join them when the customer service bell rang. Sam saw Supervisor Wallace waiting and fiddle footing in place, as if he had been stressed out. "Hello Sir, what brings you here this early?" "Well, I got my answer back from the RR head office. The telegraph clapper got so hot that I thought it was going to melt down. The words I was called are not even in the devil's vocabulary, and I'm surprised I can even walk after all the things that were shove up—you know where. So, do mankind a favor, and never ask anyone to verify something at Pettibone's office. I was so upset that I never slept a wink last night because I expected to get a transfer order this morning to go to Wyoming and pick-up turnips— fortunately, nothing has come in yet." "Sorry if I caused you all this grief." "What's done is over with. Here are your four-lifetime traveling passes, and a draft for $1,392 which is a 20% refund on your shipping charges since you bought the business. When you pay for freight charges in the future add code #1011 and deduct 20% from the amount due. Wish me luck." "Thank you, Sir."

Sam called the meeting to order. "The first item is good news. Supervisor Wallace has authorized a 20% discount on all our freight since we started the business, and for all future freight charges. Next, as you can see construction has started. In three days, a ditch was dug, an 18-inch reinforced footing poured, a 12-inch wide 2-foot-high reinforced concrete wall has been erected, and brick laying starts today as well as laying down a concrete floor.

It is estimated to be a month's project before we can move into B-Wing."

"Applications for loader positions are coming in, and will start interviews once we have 25 pre-screened applicants. I sent a letter to Wendell Winthrop in Houston looking for May graduates in brass fabrication and machine shop. Apparently, there is a lot of interest. I sent him the starting pay of $5 a day and a list of the benefits. I pointed out that they needed to pay their housing and meals. I also said that I would pay their train tickets, hotels, and meals, if they agreed to a pre- employment interview on site. And that's it for me. Neil you're up."

"Thanks, well my story is that I need help now. I have to produce some 30 scales, priming systems, and powder measures to supply our 30 new presses with all its other parts, before moving day to B-Wing. There's only Titus, Vern, Finley. and me; and there is no way we can accomplish this feat in a month's time. Plus, without help, we won't be able to produce all the parts necessary to sell presses and accessories." Elmer asked and was given the floor.

"We have been talking and three of us have agreed to temporarily move to machining till May 1st. That's me, Paul, and Glen. Elton would stay on as brass foreman which is necessary with all the new workers. Hopefully, by May we'll be able to return to our old positions."

Amy added, "well Neil, what do you think?" "Wow, that's not only teamwork, but it's also respect for the needs of the business. Yes, and Thank You. That way, we can make these necessary parts, and we'll be able to build an inventory of press parts after we move to B-Wing."

Sam added, "I think this is a great plan, but who will supervise the loaders, especially with the new workers over the next 30 days?" Glen said, "with your supervision of the new workers, I have a loader that is ready to take over my job." "Who is that?" "Ann Smith." Neil's eyebrows went up with a smile, "really, I had no idea." Amy added, "I presume that this was all well engineered, Elmer? Is that why Ann is sitting in my office so she could hear what was transpiring in the meeting?" "Yes, may I fetch her? Afterall, she is now a foreman."

"Anything else Neil?" "Yes, we need a second more modern milling machine with new cutters. Can we buy it?" "Of course." "Great, I'll give Irene the model numbers after the meeting. And last, let me read you a letter from Lionel Lofton." *Greetings Neil, it's been a while, but it was nice to hear you were working at Texas Load. I will cover your three issues individually. First, you cannot make drawing dies for the brass fabricator. These dies are proprietary and protected by a patent. You must order them thru the inventor—Big Blue. However, you can repair them if it can be done.*

Secondly, is the issue of the "sparkless" metal used to make the powder die, belling die and powder measure. I, along with the plant electrical engineer, and the head metallurgist, have conducted several experiments on the aluminum/nickel alloy #8229 for the powder measure and copper/nickel alloy #3392 for the belling die, and brass alloy #1020 for the receiving funnel, powder bowl, powder measuring scoop and scraping rod. We will certify that these are sparkless alloys and are safe when using black powder. We will give you a certificate for Lloyds of London.

The third issue was manufacturing standard loading dies for sale. It took the combined effort of our metallurgist and head 'boring' machinist to come to an agreement on the alloy needed to make each die: the sizing die, with its removable decapping pin, is made of general steel with a 3% carbon hardened sizing and radiused entry donut. The powder measure, belling die and powder die are as mentioned above. The seating die is a soft aluminum/copper alloy. The crimping die is also a 1% carbon hardened die for roll or taper crimping. I mention all this because you can see that making loading dies is not simple. Now, boring the sizing and crimping dies requires very sophisticated tools which we had to make. In short, it is not worth your time to make loading dies. We can make them because of our large machine shop, and we can make them economically—plus we provide a 100% lifetime guarantee.

As a business proposal, the powers to be and bean counters are offering you a special package. We will pour a frame and include a set of dies per your choice of caliber for $16 ($11 for the frame, and $5 for the dies)—as long as we get 100% of your year's business, for a renewal arrangement each January 1ˢᵗ. We can offer you this deal, because we all think you have a winning product. Enclosed is a contract needing Sam and Amy's signature. If you agree, we'll take your first order of 100 frames/dies or more by telegram. PS. Our electrician feels very strong that any cast iron press should be grounded with a copper wire on its base and the frame around the tool head. Respectfully, Lionel Lofton.

A long pause occurred. Amy finally said, "I think this is a good deal. Buying those loading dies that cheaply will allow our machinists to finally get ahead." Sam asked, "does anyone disagree?" Silence and negative nods later, Sam said, "then it's a deal. We'll sign the contract and have Irene put in the order."

"Amy you're up." "I've not heard a thing from Lloyds of London. I've scheduled a professional photographer for next week. We are already getting orders all over Texas. And things are somewhat stable on the processing tables. Once the photographs are done and heading to the print shop, we are going to start working on the RED BULLET-IN catalog with the products for sale. We'll need a product description, and operator's manual, do's and don'ts, loading tips, and tips on how to make black powder loading safe." "So, who will perform this job? Not worked out yet, but I'm on it. That's it for me."

"Well Irene, you're up. "I've placed orders on all our loading components—I'm trying to build our inventory before the second wave of loaders go online. I've done a complete shop inventory. We are low on everything from 'privacy papers' to every box we use in the shop. I have orders everywhere, and Cyrus and I will pick up whatever we can find in town."

"Neil and I are meeting this afternoon in the steel room. We are going over every basic steel and alloy we'll be using, and how much to keep on inventory. This morning I'm going to the new telegraph office in the park and will order the milling machine and cutters that Neil needs. I will send a telegram to Mister Lofton and order 200 frames with loading dies. The choice of dies will include, in order of immediate need: 101—38 sp., 33—44 sp., 33--45 Long Colt, and 33--44-40. Although the gun shops can load black powder in all four dies, our shop will continue only loading smokeless powder in 38s and 44s. After the inventory with Neil, I should be able to help at the processing tables today."

With everyone covered, Sam was about to close the meeting when he added, "I forgot to mention, that we are extending our market to Denver Colorado. For this expansion, we'll be using a Dallas salesman, on the job, in every gun shop in Denver. His name is Ike Webb, and I'll be training him to load, before he heads north. See you all next Friday."

Sam spent the morning with Ike. He went thru the basics of loading, and showed him the proper steps in using a press without a powder measure or a priming system. After the lunch break, Ike would be loading rounds till he got proficient. At the end of the day, Sam said, "till I get you a traveling case for this press with all the tools and components, I'd like you to come at the shop and continue loading. Irene will also show you all the other products you'll be asked to peddle along with the press. However, you won't be selling the powder measure, scale, or priming system. The operators need to learn the basic manual techniques in loading black powder ammo before getting automated.

That afternoon, Sam was planning to spend some crucial time with Bert Holiday as the construction was well on its way.

***

CHAPTER 2

Expansion and Growth

Sam walked into the construction site and Bert came to greet him. "At this point we have a reinforced footing and a 2-foot wall, all back filled and ready to lay brick. The six masons are well separated and each one is responsible for his own layers. As you can see, there is a lot of checking with the level to maintain a perfectly vertical wall. While these brick layers and their assistants are working, my other team will now build the concrete floor. In two days, we'll have the floor in and polished smooth."

"Sounds good. What is your next step?" "We'll frame in 10-foot interior walls and secure them vertically plum with temporary ceiling cross pieces till we can build trusses. These framed walls are independent of the brick walls except for the shimming two-inch blocks that abut the two walls and keeps them together. The framing will be built in 20-foot sections with a vapor barrier and 1-inch insulation board nailed on before lifting the section up. During this time, I have a team that is prebuilding 21-foot trusses, and another team that is building 8-foot loading benches, 8-foot-long brass fabrication tables, and 4X4 foot tables for the machining areas." "Why 4X4 tables?" "Because the machinists want their machines to sit 90 degrees to the main aisle with tables on the aisle end and the motors on the wall end." "I see, whereas the brass machines have five men, instead of one, working on each machine, and need the opposite layout. Great, I'll keep checking on your progress."

Sam realized he had some free time. After checking how Ann was doing, he decided to put his skills to work till he had other duties to do. So, Sam joined the machinists, and Neil gave him a part to fabricate. By the end of the first day, Sam was worn out because he had not done manual work for weeks. Sam persisted and for the next two more days, Sam managed to design, drill and thread 15 toolheads ready for loading dies. By Wednesday afternoon, things started buzzing.

The telegraph messenger arrived with a nice telegram from President Winthrop.

From Wendell Winthrop, Houston Texas

Have four fabricators and three machinists interested STOP

All planned May graduates STOP

All wish an interview ASAP STOP

All single good natured students STOP

Highly recommend each one STOP

Will arrive Sunday 3PM STOP

Please provide housing and meals STOP

All have return tickets for Wednesday STOP

Suggest getting employment contracts ready STOP

Good luck, Wendell

Sam showed Amy the telegram as she smiled and said, "that is fantastic. Now you're done machining, tomorrow I have a preselected group of 35 applicants ready for their physical performance test and that eliminating presentation of duties. Plus Dad got a notice thru the freight office that we are getting two large crates today from the Houston Foundry and two large crates from 'General Supplies.' Neil has been notified and he said he had plenty of press parts to get enough presses ready for the Friday training session. Irene is also ready for her two crates from General Supplies." "Ok, then let's close up and go home."

Setting foot in the house, Amy was quick as a cat with a HIP. "Whoa, what brought that on?" "I'm two days before my monthly and I'm checking to see if your 'pa-ding' died or something!" "Why?" "Because you haven't touched me in the past five days. I am a very 'high urge' wife and I need to be loved!" "Yes, but if you keep with your assiduous solicitude, this 'pa-ding' will start spitting, heh?" "Well, you see, it's like this. I don't need much foreplay today. I'm getting you to match my brimming state." "Enough talk, I got the message." Sam picked up his wife, locked the front door, and headed for their bedroom for an "assiduous solicitude performance."

The next day started early. Arriving at 7AM there was already a large gathering outside the shop's front door. The coffee was started, and a social get-together was started as the Duo began their physical tests. If someone passed the test, they returned to the lunchroom with the gathering. If not, they left the shop. Eight applicants failed for one or more of the four parameters—yet a hand tremor or poor coordination was the major cause for failure, with rare failures for memory, vision, or power control pushing in primers.

After the 10 o'clock break, Sam started the elimination presentation. On the first issue, where this was a one-man production and not a team effort, three applicants got up and left. Afterwards, there was a scattering of people getting up to leave. When it was mentioned that women would do the same work and pay, two men got up with an arrogant swagger. The Duo was super glad to see such characters get up and leave. The only other category that always seems to hit a nerve was the one regards hiring black or Mexican people—as usual. At the end, the Duo looked at the fifteen remaining applicants, and realized that they were all young single women of differing nationalities, and all the legal age of 18. After the usual Q & A session, Amy finally asked why this group turned out to be all women. One gal got up and said, "we are all high school graduates that cannot find a job in town unless we waitress, clean houses or sew. We are all more capable than that, and we want a future where we can earn our own money to help support our family—yes, we are all looking for a man in our lives." "Then, start looking, there are plenty of eligible men in the brass fabrication unit, and we'll have seven more applicants on Monday from Houston. Look your best Monday morning, because we'll have a social hour 8-10AM, an hour at lunch, and an hour at 4PM to allow people to meet and introduce themselves."

Sam finished the presentation by explaining the wages of $4 a day with 50 cent increases at 1,500 and 2,000 pieces loaded per day. If the applicants worked out, they would make $5 a day like all the workers and with all the employment benefits. "Tomorrow, Amy and I will be beginning your training—remember, only short sleeve shirts or blouses."

After the applicants left, Amy conducted the biweekly payday. Afterwards, Sam, Neil, Elmer and Glen got together and set up all fifteen new presses with powder measures and priming systems. All fifteen were set with either 38 target or hot loads. While the boys were at work, Irene and Ann were waiting for their husbands. Irene decided to talk to Amy.

"Now that I'm use to this job, it seems that I get everything done by the 2:45 break. I then spend the rest of the day at the processing tables. Now, don't take me wrong, I like working with Ida and Lucille, but maybe I can be more productive doing something else." "Like what?" "Like start writing all those catalog product descriptions, operator manuals, do's and don'ts, loading tips, and how-to make loading black powder safe." "I know about your mastery of the English composition, and I realize that you have mastered the use of all these tools, but I just couldn't find the words to ask you to take this over, seeing how you just started the purchasing/inventory job." "Well, I'll be glad to do it, and will accept anyone's ideas on the subject."

*

The next day started with a social hour outside the doors as the Duo arrived. Once the fifteen new workers were divided into two groups, the Duo started the training. By the 10AM break, the workers were getting the gist of things. Starting to load on their own, the group was ordered to follow the steps per the called-out directions. Within the hour, the new workers were let loose. Ann joined the Duo in supervising five new workers. By lunchtime, it was clear that several new loaders were getting comfortable and producing some perfect ammo.

By 3PM, Sam was able to leave the beginners to Ann and Amy. Sam was meeting with the electrician to lay out the ceiling lights over four new rows. The meeting started and the four lanes were measured off the wall. At that point, Sam wanted a light every two benches plus a light at each end of the rows, and four lights over the aisles. The electrician surprised Sam when he said that he wanted to remove all the existing single and two-phase knob-and-tube wires, and lay all new wires for the ceiling lights. The reason given was that the old wires had heated so much that they became a fire hazard. Apparently, the new wires planned for B-Wing had a wire sheath with a higher heat insulation and resistance. The electricians would be pulling the single-phase wires and installing new wires for ceiling lights, leaving the working double phase till moving day.

Saturday was a rest day for the Duo. Spent at home, Amy busied herself with cooking meals ahead of time, doing laundry, and cleaning. Sam picked up the vittles and fresh meat for the week, ran errands at the bank and post office, and paid bills. By supper time, the Duo was in their tub getting ready for dining and dancing.

Their table was finally full with Elmer and Lucille joining the Studgards, Balingers, Holts, and Smiths. After a chicken pie supper, the dancing started. Everyone seemed to be having a grand time. It was Sam who commented to Amy, "we are so fortunate to have such friends. I would never hesitate to trust any one of them with our lives." "I agree."

The next morning, the Duo got up late and had a brunch at 11AM. After lounging around, the Duo then made arrangements with the local taxi service to send two carriages to pick up the students from Houston College. The Duo was waiting on the train platform when all seven men disembarked with their two carpetbags. Sam and Amy greeted them and escorted them to the Industrial Hotel located in the park.

"You have two double rooms and a triple. Your meals in the hotel restaurant are all included. You have a five minute walk to our shop—the TEXAS LOAD. Get familiar with the adjoining Dallas suburb which is where most workers live. Tomorrow join us at 7AM, and Amy will introduce you to our other workers. The individual interviews and your work capabilities will be checked out afterwards. Tuesday is a free day for you to enjoy, but you need to decide if you want the job and live in Dallas—I need to know either way before you leave."

The Duo had cinnamon rolls and coffee ready when they opened the doors. It was clear that couples were quickly forming as the two-hour introductions moved along. With the loaders going to their benches, the four brass fabricators were put to work making 38 sp. brass. Elton like their techniques and gave all four a thumbs up. Neil gave the three machinists a part to make by using the new milling machine. The three workers were pleased to see such a modern machine, and all excelled in making the assigned part. Neil was surprised to see young men smile as they worked. Having all passed the competency portion. The Duo decided to conduct private interviews to get names, ages, and personal facts. The Duo was somewhat surprised to find out what was the major drive to move to Dallas. The truthful answers always covered four things. First, a raving recommendation from Professor Winthrop who felt that Sam and Amy would be the best bosses they could ever find. The TEXAS LOAD was offering a better than a living wage and great benefits. It was also a shop where they could practice their learned trade, and they hired young single women, which was rare in a man's factory world. "Tomorrow is your personal day, take a taxi on my bill, and have him drive you in this suburb and thru the big city, or hang around the shop, or do what you like. As I previously said, I expect you to decline our offer or accept it and sign a contract by 5PM. Oh, by the way, all the new loader workers will be getting out of work by lunchtime in case you want to have lunch with someone, heh."

*

The next day, with five contracts in hand for brass fabricators and three for machinists, the search was now completed. Boarding houses were alerted of the incoming business by May, and any reservation that was available was taken up by the Duo.

Starting the next Monday morning, Sam went to see the B-Wing's progress. Bert surprised him with a traveling box. Ike, who was already busy loading, was called over. Inside the box was a progressive press with several padded bunkers and several removable retaining blocks. The toolhead/ dies was already in place, and above the dies was a drawer for primers, cases, and lead bullets. The black powder was in a secure brass flask, isolated from the primers. There was also a slot for the RED BULLET-IN. Ike kept staring, pulled the unit out, checked all the storage and finally said, "This is perfect for traveling by train and local buggy. I'm ready, so when do I start?" "For now, I need to see how close we are to moving, and how the RED BULLET-IN is coming along. You need the bulletin as part of your sales pitch. So, until it is ready, you might as well continue loading."

Sam then turned to Bert, "so where are we up to?" "As you can see, the trusses are up with their floor supports, the brick walls are done, and the steel roof will be up in two days. Then we panel the ceilings, insulate them as the panels go up, paint them white, and the electricians will be laying out the wires for the four rows of ceiling lights. We'll be paneling the walls and installing all the windows next. Again, after painting the walls grey, the electricians will follow us and lay the knob-and-tube wires for two-phase service to a wall outlet for all your motorized machines. During all this, we'll be building those rooms at the end of the wing for power/furnace, storage, and your press processing center." "How long before we can move in?" "Give us two complete weeks, and you'll be doing the big move."

Amy was listening to Bert's outline, and realized that it was crucial to get this bulletin out for Ike to get to work. Amy then called Irene and Luke in their office. The first question was to Luke, "how is that young man you hired working out?" "Kent Knowles is a very efficient and polite individual. He's quickly picked up the job, and is already functioning independently." "Where did you find him?" "He's a local boy who has worked for the past two years as a clerk in the hardware store. He makes $4 a day and is satisfied since he lives at home." "Well, if he can perform your job for the next five days, we'll increase his wages to $5." "Ok, that means that I'm going to be doing something different for a week, heh?"

"Yes, and that depends on Irene and me." Amy went into detail why the RED BULLET-IN had to be done this week— "we're moving in two weeks, and Ike needs the bulletin to go to work in Denver." "Irene jumped in and said, I have the press's operator manual finished, Glen has the scale's manual done, and is almost ready with the priming system's manual. We have to write a content page, loading tips, do's and don'ts, and how to load black powder safely." Amy added, "if I join you, and we both work on this full time, we'll have this done and printed by Friday." Luke added, "and I presume I'm going to be working your printing press full time this week, heh?" "Yes, and I have 200 pages of each photographed tool ready for adding the written data. Also, here is the 'content page' which I've been adding to for months." Luke read Irene's press manual and then Amy's content page:"

CONTENT PAGE

1. Press. 2. Powder measure. 3. Priming system. 4. Loading dies in 38, 44, 45LC, and 44-40. 5. Balance beam scale. 6. Tool kit. 7. Replacement small parts. 8. Pickup tubes. 9. Extra toolheads. 10. Brass scoop kit for BP. 11. Replacement brass funnel. 12. Safety spectacles. 13. Extra decapping pins. 14. Steel C-Arm individual press with universal decapping die. 15. Dismantling collet pliers per caliber. 16. Important articles—Do's and Don'ts of loading, loading tips, and how to make loading BP safe. Plus, several order forms at the end of the catalog."

Luke had his work cut out, so he went to work. Amy took over the article on how to make BP safe as Irene started on loading tips. Sam, who had watched and listened to the Trio's plans, simply smiled and went to assist Ann in supervising all those new loaders. By the end of the day, Amy's article was done as Irene started to proofread the results.

HOW TO LOAD BP SAFELY

1. This is a manual process with the use of brass scoops by 'volume' to add powder instead of a powder measure, and a finger pickup of primers without the use of an automatic priming system. Scale not needed.

2. The powder die(not powder measure) is made for BP use. The die (aluminum/copper), the belling adapter (copper/nickel), and the receiving funnel (brass). These are all 'sparkless' metals safe when loaded with BP.

3. Ground your press. Use a 12-gauge copper wire tied to a steel water pipe (not a lead pipe) or to a 4-foot-deep underground grounding rod. Attach the wire to the press's base, and

wrap it around the powder die itself just below the receiving funnel.

4. Follow basic operator precautions. Wear protective spectacles, never smoke while loading, do not wear woolen clothing, wear shoes with leather soles, stand on a wooden floor, sit on wooden bench, and grab the grounding wire as you approach the loading press—to clear your body of surface electricity that can spark and ignite BP.

5. Never take your hat off to scratch your head. That will energize your fingers to spark on contact. If you do, then de-electrify your fingers by grabbing the ground wire.

Irene was still adding to her long list of loading tips, so Amy went to check on her dad's progress. He was still setting type on a separate frame as the machine was printing away the press's operator manual.

The next day, Irene finished her long list of loading tips, as Amy was hard at work on the "Do's and Don'ts."

LOADING TIPS

1. Don't push a primer in once the powder is added. 2. Never pump a primer—push it in to its stop. 3. Oil hinges and Ram every 2 hours. 4. Check loaded round for high primers or fabricating error and place in dismantling pot. 5. Check your powder charge twice a day. 6. Don't load a deformed lead bullet. 7. Use your powder measure 'knocker' every round to completely empty the powder cavity. 8. Fill your pickup tubes, between 4 and 5PM, before leaving the shop. 9. Before filling your pickup tubes, look for primers that are missing the anvil, and discard them. 10. Periodically check the priming push rod for debris that will mar the primer's surface. 11. Always use your spectacle's brush to clean off metal specks before washing them. 12. Always keep control of the processing handle—never let the platform crash down. 13. Every 500 rounds clean your seating and crimping die of accumulated lead debris—to avoid deep seating or over crimping. 14. Apply the bullet on top of the case and within 30 degrees of vertical, or it won't go in. 15. Keep your powder measure half full at all times. Learn how many rounds it will take to get to half—if you ever run your press

dry, stop, and see your foreman—someone will be dismantling a lot of rounds. 16. Don't load a 'dud' or 'squib' as it's called on the range. If unsure, look inside before you add the bullet. If bullet is already on, set it aside for later dismantling.

Amy had just finished her list and showed it to Irene. They both realized that some of the issues were a repeat from other lists, but elected to leave on this final list in the catalog as a reminder of the crucial issues in loading live ammo.

DO'S AND DON'TS

1. Never push a high primer once the powder is added.
2. The powder measure and priming system is only for smokeless powder.
3. Always wear eye protection.
4. Never force a primer that won't go in. It will go off if you persist.
5. Never load a smokeless powder charge greater than the published data.
6. Never smoke while loading.
7. If reloading 'once fired brass,' add the decapping pin to the sizing die.

8. Never compress any powder—the higher pressure can be devastating.
9. Never leave powder in a powder measure overnight. If not loading, it belongs in the original powder container to avoid changes in moisture content and other oxidizing changes.
10. Keep unused primers in the original tin or the pickup tubes to avoid moisture damage—even if just overnight.

At that point, Irene continued working on writing descriptions of the other many products listed in the catalog. The major one that had been forgotten was the step-by-step process of adjusting the four loading dies. Amy, on the other hand, went to help Ida and Lucille on the processing tables, as Luke was busy setting type and printing 200 copies of each page in the catalog.

*

For the next week, Sam spent most of his time supervising the new batch of loaders. His only break was when he went to the bank to make the daily deposits. By Thursday he decided to have a private chat with Amy. "Amy, the deposits are unbelievably large. I suspect we are making too much money. Why is that?" "Well our cost of goods is stable or low, our labor is the same, and our overhead expenses are also stable. The biggest savings is because we make our own brass cartridges and save 2/3 of the cost for casings—and besides, there is no brass cartridge supplier that would be able to supply our needs. We have a firm contract with a Missouri mining company to provide us unlimited hardcast 38 and 44 bullets for the next two years. The powder companies have a surplus of smokeless powder and will deliver any amount of fast and medium burning powder we want."

"The only component that is fragile is primers." We've been fortunate to get all the primers we want thru Winchester. But yesterday I got this letter and contract from Ira. Basically, if we supply Winchester a RR 300 lb. crate of 30-30 casings each month, we'll get a 2-year contract for unlimited primers at a 10% reduction over current prices. Plus we'll still get 11 cents per casing and Winchester pays for shipping to Connecticut."

"Well, from what I see, this sounds like a good deal for us. Let's break it down. How many casings is 300 pounds of 30-30s and how long does it take our fabricators to put out this order?" "Ok, here goes. Follow my math. First let's work up the income.

30-30s weigh 19 pounds per thousand casings.

50-pound case = 2,600 casings = $260 (11 cents minus 1 cent for the brass buds).

Six 50-pound cases = 300-pound RR crate, or 15,600 casings- which is worth $1,560 in gross income for us."

"Secondly, let's work up the manpower to produce a 300lb. RR crate. Keep in mind that a 30-30 casing requires a bit more work than a 38 special.

One operator = +-1000 casings a day.

Three operators = 3,000 casings per day.

Since we need 15,600 casings for 300 lbs. Then 15,600 ÷ 3,000 = +- 5 days for 3 operators to put out 300 pounds of 30-30 casings—plus we make +- $1,500.

"Wow, it's a no-brainer. Let's sign the contract. I will notify Ira by telegram that we'll ship Winchester a 300-pound crate the first of each month, and mail him the signed contract. Now, since we're doing some computations, lets see what our production is and why our deposits are so high." "Ok, again follow my math. Let say we have 10 loaders that need 10 men producing 38 and 44 casings—for a total of a 20-man team.

10 loaders = 20,000 loaded rounds/day (2,000 rounds/man) or that's 100,000 loaded rounds a week, or 1.3 million per 13-week quarter, or +-5 million loaded rounds/year.

5,000,000 casings ÷ 50 rounds per box = 100,000 fifty-round ammo boxes per year. Now figure an average of $2.75 a box, that's an amazing gross income of +-$270,000 per year."

"Labor expenses.

Each man makes $25 a week multiply by 52 weeks = $1,300 a year.

$1,300 multiplied by 20 men = $26,000 a year in labor costs."

"Cost of goods, depreciation, and other overhead expenses.

Let's stay with $1.80 a box like in the past. 100,000 boxes at $1.80 is $180,000. Add depreciation of $12,000 a year and overhead costs at $17,000 a year and you have:

$270,000, -$26,000, -$180,000, -$12,000, -$17,000, EQUALS $35,000 of profit per year. BUT, if you use 30 loaders and say 20 fabricators, then your profit is multiplied by threefold to +-$100,000." "And that is ridiculous, we have no business making this kind of money." "I agree, so why not give more to our employees. You realize that we'll be about 60 employees strong by the six-month mark just before the July vacation—that's assuming we keep the loading force at 30 workers. If we go to 40 loaders, then we'll be at our maximum of 70 employees." "Either way, we'll be giving some amazing bonuses at our end of June meeting, heh?"

*

A week later two things happened that changed things around. Luke finished printing and arranging together 200 RED BULLET-IN, and Bert had five days of work left to be done B-Wing. The Duo read thru the entire bulletin, and were surprised to find a detailed order on how to set loading dies. With a perfect bulletin, Ike was called to the office.

"Well Ike, we are moving in a week, and the bulletin is ready. If you're ready, then it's time to head to Denver and start your career as a TEXAS LOAD salesman." "I'm ready and looking forward to the challenge. My wife is also prepared, and this is a big step for us. Now give me your priorities." "Ok, well selling our ammo is your #1 job.

Package A—4cases of 38's =96 boxes X $2.50 = $240 = 4,800 rounds,

Package B—4 cases of 44's=64boxes X $3.00= $192 = 4,000 rounds.

"The second job is to introduce them to our Black Powder 'Reloading' press. Emphasize a 'Reloading' press of once or more fired brass casings. Go thru the entire demonstration of loading the press, do a few loaded rounds, then show them how to close down the press. Leave a RED BULLET-IN, tell them the press will be 'coming soon.' Emphasize they can have one per gun shop because it is for their own use and not for sale. Also repeatedly remind them that this is a Black Powder unit, and the powder measure, priming system, and scale are not for sale at this time. They are for the future when smokeless powder will become available."

Amy added, "we're not after getting a deposit, but if someone insists on pre-paying for one press and the accessories, well we can't refuse. So give them a receipt and add that the press is still 6-weeks today from coming to the market—and change the weeks as they go by. The price for a press with one set of dies is $45. An accessory package of $10 includes, a toolbox, small parts kit, brass scoop kit and bowl/scraper, and safety spectacles. Other parts are extra:

- Extra 4-die set = $8 (choice of 38, 44, 45Long Colt, or 44-40).
- Extra toolhead = $5.
- Steel C-Arm press with universal decapping die = $15.
- Universal decapping die = $3. (can be used with extra toolhead)
- Dismantling collet pliers = $2."

"When you get to Denver, deposit this $250. First buy a horse and buggy, and use the balance for your livery fees, housing, meals, and miscellaneous expenses. Make a bank deposit after two gun shop purchases or $500. Don't carry any more money than that. Wire us your bank balance each Friday. Always keep enough in the bank to cover your expenses. You work M-F as previously discussed, unless a weekend day is necessary. We have 200 RED BULLET-IN for you and enough components to get you thru the 100-gun shops in Denver. We prefer you wear a handgun. Good luck, and be careful." "I always wear my pistol. I'll be back in two weeks and we can discuss how many days off

I'll need. An entire week as you suggested is too much."

After Ike left, the Duo went to see Bert. The carpenters were doing finish work. A team was building shelves and worktables in the storage rooms and Irene was there directing what she needed for the press processing center. Neil worked on getting his steel/alloy racks built and Glen was directing his brass fabricating shelves. Bert came over and said "my boys, after talking to Neil and Glen, feel that there will be too much dust in B-Wing. We all think we should put two ceiling exhaust fans on each side of B-Wing to keep the air fresh and free of metal dust." "Of course, go ahead, now's the time to do it before you finish the ceiling."

"So, are we still scheduled for a Monday move?" "Yes, Sir. We'll be out of here lock stock and barrel come Friday night." "Good, but you do good work. Bring me your final bill and we'll settle then."

"Well, dear, do we move Saturday, or wait till Monday?" "Wait till Monday, we have dinner and dancing Saturday night, and that has become a very important event for our hardworking friends, heh?" "Yes, you're right. Monday it is."

***

CHAPTER 3

The Move and More

During the weekend, the electricians came and pulled all the two-phase knob-and-tube wires. So, come Monday, the brass fabricators and machine shop tools could be moved to B-Wing. As prearranged, the loaders stayed home to avoid a traffic jam.

Neil, along with Elmer, Titus, Vern, Finley, and Paul started pulling the machining tools from their concrete anchors. They had a dozen machines to free up and move them, along with two machines that Neil took out of storage. Once free, four men lifted the machine and moved it in one piece to its new home. There the electricians were waiting to connect the motors to the wall outlets and copper grounding wire. The last part was to drill the concrete and insert concrete anchors to stabilize the machining tool. Once the tool was all set into place, the carpenters brought in each tool's own 4X4 ft. end table and added some wall shelves for miscellaneous items. Luke then brought in each machine's toolbox and cutting oil. By lunch time, the job was done as Kent cleaned the old machining site in A-Wing.

On the fabricating side, Glen was supervising some 20 men do the same. The brass fabrication machines needed dismantling in five parts, which were the parts controlled by each man of the 5-men team of fabricators. Not only did they have to dismantle them, but they had to reassemble them before anchoring them to the concrete floor. It took two men to carry 1/5th of each fabricating machine. Once the five pieces were reassembled and reattached together, the electricians electrified and grounded each motor. The last step was to anchor each machine to the concrete like it was done on the machine shop side. The carpenters added the matching 8-foot table and also added some wall shelves. Luke finished supplying the brass fabricators with the cleaning agents, oils, and hand tools needed. An ample supply of brass buds was left at each 5-man machine. Once the four fabricating machines were installed, there was enough space left over for two more machines—for future growth.

By lunch time, B-Wing had new permanent tenants. The afternoon would be spent at full operations to confirm that each machine was level and working properly. The electricians would monitor the power distribution to verify adequate voltage and rule out the overheating of defective wires.

During lunch, Amy was on the prowl. She finally confirmed that some of the single brass fabricators had already paired with the 'second wave' single female loaders. Sam said, "boy, that didn't take long. I wonder if the new college recruits might already have paired with the other leftover single gals?" "Oh yeah, my spies already confirmed that each of those 'second wave' gals were writing regularly to those college boys." "Oh my, what have we done, we're going to end up with a maternity ward of pregnant gals." "Nonsense, we'll give all of them our 'safe sex' talk, and buy some time. Not to worry, we'll manage, heh?"

By the end of lunch, the 30 loaders were arriving with their cardboard box. Each loader was instructed to empty their loading bench down to the anchored press. The carpenters arrived with multiple wagons full of 8-foot-long loading benches with one side plate and a backwall with shelves. Four rows of 10 loading benches were set up under the new row of ceiling lights. Row 1 and 2 were back-to-back with an ample aisle between them for the expediters to fit their wagon. Row 3 and 4 were also back-to-back with an aisle between each row. Of note is that row 2 and 3 had their benches touching back-to-back. Each row ended up with overhead ceiling lights as well as ceiling lights over the aisles. These four rows occupied 26 feet wide, thereby leaving enough room for the expediter wagons to get to the side wall storage rooms.

The supervisor's double bench without any backing or side plates, was placed perpendicular and across Row 2 and 3, thereby allowing visibility to all four rows. The left side of the supervisor's bench had a C-Arm frame with a decapping die and collet dismantling priers, whereas the right side had a functional loading press.

Ida and Lucille were rearranging the processing tables to match the new 'loading row' setups. Carpenters were building Amy a new mailing table, set off to the side, with wide shelving against the wall. This would allow Ida and Lucille to fill 50-pound fixed rate boxes and place them on the holding shelves till Amy got to them to fill out the orders. This change cut down the congestion on the processing tables, and allowed more room for Irene when she came to help.

With the new distribution of loading benches and processing tables, it became clear that there was a total of 15 X 40 feet at the end of A-Wing that was totally unused. Sam met with Luke and quickly decided that the space would be used for storage of lead bullets and other supplies when the storage rooms were full. At the present growth, it would become an issue as soon as the next batch of 100 progressive press frames arrived. So the 600 square feet of space was tentatively reserved for lead bullets.

By 4PM, the move was completed, and B-Wing had been operating all afternoon without problems. The wiring was certified as safe and operational with adequate grounding of each machine and its motors. With everyone gathering in the lunchroom, Sam started the meeting.

"Thank you everyone for a job well done. It will be 'all hands on deck' tomorrow morning. I think you'll find the new working digs to be a bit more user friendly. So, here we are, the third and last time we enlarged the lunchroom. We are about +-60 in attendance, and if we fill the last 10 loading positions, we'll +-70 employees. The one positive comment is the new water fountain next to the lunchroom—so enjoy."

"Next, I'd like to discuss what our different needs will be between now and May when we get a manpower boost in the machine shop and brass fabrication sections."

"First, as you know, Ike Webb is in Denver and we expect an influx of new orders. To meet that demand, I ask the following. Elton, keep three machines making 38 sp. cartridges, and one machine making 44 sp. cartridges. One of the 38 sp. machines will be designated to make Winchester's full 300-pound crate of 30-30's for the first week of each month. The distribution balance should work, unless demand from Colorado changes things."

"Now Ann, unless things change, set your 30 current machines' powder measures as such:

Fifteen 38 Target—3.5 grain of fast burning powder = 750fps.

Eight 38 Hot—5.0 grain of fast burning powder = 950fps.

Four 44 Target—5.0 grain of medium burning powder = 750fps.

Three 44 Hot—7.5 grain of medium burning powder = 950fps."

"Neil, thanks to your team's hard work we have 40 progressive loading presses in A-Wing. So from now on, build press accessory parts and get presses ready for boxing. Hold up on fabricating scales, priming systems or powder measures since we will be selling only Black Powder manual presses once the ammo buying rush from Denver quiets down."

"Irene, contact Big Blue and order the fifth 5-man machine in 38 special, but when it is being set up, have the technician put in the 30-30 dies to free up the 38 special machine, and avoid changing dies once a month. At the same time, order two full 5 stage drawing dies for the new cartridge 45ACP—for future speculation. This being a new caliber, there may be a long wait which is Ok, since we're not ready for it."

"You know we're making money, so plan on a bonus at the June business meeting before the July vacation. Now, please don't advertise this to the public. I have a reason for this, and will explain it further at our meeting."

"The last item, as a precaution, if ever Amy and I have to leave suddenly for whatever reason, then someone has to become the temporary manager in charge with all rights to conduct business. Amy and I toiled over this for many days since we have eight very capable foremen. Yet there is only one that is trained or has experience in all six fields, plus has access to your payroll distribution. Those shop division are: brass fabrication, machining, loading, processing, purchasing, and office management. Yes, you've all guessed who I'm referring to. That is Irene Holt. Loud Applause and congratulations followed. See you all tomorrow," as several people came over to personally congratulate her— including her proud husband.

*

A week later things were becoming routine. All three sections were at full production and orders were already coming in from Denver. Every order was twice to triple the usual Texas orders. In addition, every gun shop was ordering and prepaying for a BP press with the accessory kit. Sam commented, "it's obvious that the age of smokeless powder has arrived. Even in Denver there seems to be a shortage of this type of ammo, and it is all to our advantage—for the time to make hay is when the sun shines. Colt and other gun manufacturers are putting out VP firearms and people are tired of cleaning the caustic nature of BP fouling. So we have a short time frame before smokeless powder hits the retail market, and soon we'll add our BP presses before that market disappears."

As Amy was thinking of this, all hell broke out. It sounded like the town was invaded. Gunshots were exploding everywhere on Main Street.

Sam, Amy, and Glen grabbed their pistols and ran outside. Cyrus who had been running errands, was just arriving on his buggy, as the Trio jumped in and Cyrus raced to the gunfight. By the time they arrived, the result was evident. Sheriff Wilson was holding a bloody arm and two pedestrians were on the ground, being attended to by Doc Kipp. Heading to the bank an obvious robber, next to the bank steps, was dead on the ground. Once inside, a cashier was dead as President Cunningham was on the floor next to the open vault—with a bloodied face, he had obviously been pistol-whipped.

"Well Grover how did it happen and how much was taken?" Six men rushed in and demanded I unlock the vault. When I refused, they pistol-whipped me and shot my old cahier, Ransom Grant, and killed him. Afterwards they threatened to kill another cashier or customer every 10 seconds unless

I opened the vault. They emptied us out to the tune of $60,000 and our customers will lose everything except the 15% we get from the parent company for everyone's accounts. Sam this is serious, you have $50,000 in the bank, so unless we get the money back, you will get $7,500 for your account and this branch will permanently close."

"Grover, that's only money, people have died here. As they left, did they take any hostage?" "Oh my God, that poor gal!" "Who was that?" "Melanie Foxworth was the only customer at the time, and they took her out under gunpoint." "That's why the dead outlaw's horse is gone."

"Melanie was riding him. Has someone sent word to Sil yet?" "No, I don't think so." A local rancher volunteered to head out to Sil's ranch and do the dreaded messaging—as the man was asked to tell Sil to meet at Bidwell's Mercantile.

The Trio went outside to check with Sheriff Wilson. "Charlie and I were having breakfast when the first shot was heard. We both went outside, but an outlaw was standing in the street with a rifle in hand. He was waiting for us. I took a slug in the arm, but Charlie put him down with his pump shotgun. As Charlie was helping me up, the gang came out, all six of them, shooting anything in sight. People were dropping to the ground as we also did. They then got away, except for that one."

"Well sheriff, we'll go after them." "Charlie can go with you!" "No, with you out of commission, he'll be the only law left in town. Instead, let's find Wil, when Sil arrives, we'll be enough to track this outfit down."

The Trio went to pick up their pump shotguns and their 30-30's, along with their winter gear and personals. They then rode their horses and Wilbur with his packsaddle to Asa's store. Glen was picking up spare ammo and basic cooking utensils, Amy was picking out vittles, as Sam was adding bear and wolf traps.

By the time the Trio was ready to ride, Sil arrived with another rider.

Sam and Amy took a good look at the older gentlemen—an Indian, with jet black hair, dark eyes, the reddish complexion, and the face of an older Sil. Looking back at Sil, and back at the older Indian, Sil added, "I know you know, his name is 'Two Cloud,' and we'll talk about that later, right now I want my wife back. This man is the best tracker you'll ever find." "Great, let's ride!"

The tracks were easy to follow till they set cross country. That's when Two Cloud took a careful look at the tracks. In good English, he said, "one horse missing half a shoe. That is good for us." For another two hours, the posse followed Two Cloud. When they arrived at a stream, the trampled area had been where the outlaws had stopped to water their horses. Two Cloud was smelling around and could smell human and horse urine. As he stepped off in the bushes, he returned and said, "Melanie carrying my grandchild. Must rescue her tonight before she gets dehydrated. One long day in saddle is all she can safely take—mount up." Sil added, this must be early, because we did not know."

How Two Cloud could follow tracks in the long grasses at a slow gallop was unbelievable, but he never lost his way. It was getting dark when he stopped and claimed to be smelling camp smoke. No one else could smell the smoke but Amy added, "if he can smell pregnant urine, then we better believe him and make some plans for saving Melanie."

Everyone got into moccasins. Sil was going with Two Cloud to sneak into camp once the outlaws drank themselves into a stupor. Sil was to bring a bag full of traps and lay them out next to the spot where Melanie had been restrained, and next to the horse picket line. With a full moon for ambient light, the Trio snuck to within 75 yards, and had a good scope picture of the campfire and the sleeping outlaws. The plan was to let Sil and Two Cloud rescue Melanie and boobytrap the camp—while the Trio provided a backup cover in case things went awry.

The Indian and half breed snuck up to a sleeping Melanie, when she was awakened only to see her husband's loving face. Sil and Melanie disappeared as Two Cloud went to work. The Trio was still watching Two Cloud lay out traps in both chosen locations when he disappeared and reappeared next to the pile of supplies. There he laid out several camouflaged wolf traps. To the Trio's surprise, Two Cloud was also seen dumping some dry seeds in several bottles of whiskey.

After everyone gathered, Sil was instructed to move back 200 yards with Melanie. It was then that Two Cloud was asked two questions, what did you do to the horses and what did you put in the whiskey bottle. Two Cloud started laughing. "How you know?" "Saw you in the scope!" "Oh, well, horses had been left saddled, so I loosened the cinch's buckle." "And the whiskey?" "One bead is good laxative, three beads are horse laxative plugged with colic, twelve beads is explosive nightmare—ha, ha, haaah."

The group pulled back and decided that this was not a good place to have an all-out fight in the dark. If daylight came, then the group would attack from 150 yards to keep out of range of their 1873 rifles. Unfortunately, an outlaw went to the bushes and when he returned to camp went to check on the hostage. The group, even at 150 yards, hear that unmistakable SNAP followed by a howl from hell. The entire camp was up to see what was going on. When the gang leader saw his buddy caught like a predator, and the hostage gone, he yelled, "grab the whiskey, your guns and the money. We're out of here!"

In a matter of minutes, another outlaw was caught in the wolf traps that managed to break his foot, unlike the bear trap that nearly amputated the leg of the first outlaw. Now with two disabled outlaws, the odds were getting better. The outlaws got on their horses as several were heard yelling after only a few yards at a full gallop. Two Cloud was hiding nearby and saw the result of his antics. Falling off the horses, one outlaw broke his arm, one dislocated his shoulder, and the other had a new face from scraping the ground. The gang leader, the only uninjured one, ordered the cinches tightened and off they went.

The Trio elected to wait till daylight to go after them. Two Cloud would go with them as Sil was convinced to bring his bride back to the ranch. After starting a fire and making a full breakfast, the new Quad took off after the outlaws. It was clear the outlaws were still traveling north, which meant they were heading to Gainesville where they could take a train west to Wichita Falls with a population of 5,000 people. Having traveled an estimated 30 miles yesterday, it was assumed that they had another 40 miles to the first train yard. The hunters knew they had to capture them on the trail, or spend weeks finding them in Wichita Falls—assuming they had not kept on going to unknown locations further west when they and the money would forever be gone.

The push was on, and Two Cloud was at his best. An hour later, everyone could smell human feces along the trail. It started as solid piles turning to liquid explosions. Eventually, the outlaws were camped along the trail. Two Cloud said, "I knew those idiots could not wait to drink till safe on the train. Human nature never fails."

The Quad made their way to 150 yards. In their scope, they saw most of the outlaws squatting any place there was room, and groaning with severe cramps. Included this time was the gang leader, who had probably had more liquor than the others. Two Cloud added, "these beads also make you thirsty, so they probably emptied their canteens, only to make the backdoor trots even worse. Ha, ha, haaaaaah!"

Sam took aim and pulverized a bottle of whiskey, "that does it, you're all under arrest. Put your guns down and hands up or we'll mow you down with our shotguns. Two Cloud was first to make it to camp, but never thought the gang leader would pull a cocked pistol on him. Two Cloud knew that instant, that he was about to meet his ancestors, as a shot rang out from afar. The gang leader's head exploded, and nothing was left above the eyes. By then Sam, Wil, and Glen were on site to secure the other outlaws. Amy had stayed at 150 yards as a backup defense.

After throwing the living outlaws in the nearby river, they forced them to scrub themselves with lye soap and scrub their britches clean. It was a long way home, but after camping out one night, the Quad and Two Cloud arrived at noon in Dallas. The sheriff and President Cunningham greeted them. The sheriff reported that this was the Stutler gang, out of Trinidad Colorado, who were wanted dead or alive for robbery and senseless murders. Their bounty rewards came to $7,000. It was Sam who addressed President Cunningham, "here is your $60,000 minus our 15% fee of $9,000." "But Sam, the usual 'finder's fee' is normally 10%." "Not anymore, and if you get robbed again, it's going to be 20%. So, just like the other banks in town, add some bars to the windows and hire armed guards whenever you're open. Either that, or I'm pulling my money out and changing banks. I've had enough of your anachronistic ways. It's time to modernize especially when you're dealing with industries and their large financial investments, employees and incomes."

As everyone was preparing to leave, Irene came running and jumped into Glen's arms. Afterwards, with hugs to go around, she finally hugged Amy and said, "thank God you are all safe, and you my dear can have your job back. I prefer being just a purchasing agent, heh?"

*

It took a week for the sheriff to gather all the funds, bounties, and miscellaneous cash. The entire lot was broken down as: $9,000 for finder's fee, $7,000 in bounty rewards, $1,300 in pocket cash, seven horses with tact for $750, seven pistols and rifles for $350 and miscellaneous trail items and scabbards for another $100. A total of $18,500. $500 was given to the sheriff for securing the bounties, horses and guns. The $18,000 was divided six ways—Sam, Amy, Glen, Wil, Sil and Two Cloud—gave each one $3,000.

Now two weeks since the move, the Duo was back full swing. Today, Ike Webb on his first week off, was coming to the office to discuss his two weeks' work. In preparation for the meeting, Amy had pulled the ledger on the Colorado ammo orders and all the preorders for presses. "Well Ike, you've been busy. The orders are coming out of Denver and all large orders. Tell us what the story is."

"You won't believe this, but there's big bucks and a big demand for smokeless ammunition in that city. I actually felt like I fell into in a pit where loaded ammo was more valuable than gold. Every gun shop gave me a resounding welcome and every shop owner was eager to place an order. To my surprise, the orders were large, and it seemed that the standard order was 4 Package A 38 Target, costing $960, with 2 Package B 44 Hot, costing another $384. That came to $1,344 but every gun shop I visited preordered and prepaid your progressive press with the accessory kit. That came to $1,400 and not a one even hesitated. Plus they all signed the liability release; emphasizing the smokeless ammo was only for VP certified guns, and the press was only for manually reloading BP ammo."

Sam added, "Ike are you aware what those orders came to since you visited forty gun shops in 10 working days?" "Yes, just about $56,000." Sam looked at Amy, who was monitoring the ledger, and confirmed Ike's approximate amount. Sam added, "well, Ike, I feel we need to adjust your income to reflect a more equitable commission for such sales."

Ike was prepared for that statement and jumped in before Sam got too far along. "In three weeks, I will be done with Denver's one hundred gun shops and will then move south. Those high Denver sales were a one-time sale. The future repeat orders will come from your order forms you place in each fixed rate box. Now in smaller Colorado cities there are fewer shooting clubs and less money about the towns. So orders will change with a downward trend, and end up more realistic. So to cut to the chase, I'm working for the employment benefits and the security if affords my partially disabled wife. My $5 a day is fine. Heck, I get 3 hot meals a day, all train fares paid, all business expenses paid, and I sleep in a fine hotel every night. I'm happy, the wife is very happy, and married life's benefits are at their all-time high—pardon my saying so, but there's no price for that, heh?"

Amy jumped in and added, "we know you can earn more money somewhere else, but in view of a close-knit shop, it is probably best to leave your wages where they are, and avoid silly grumbling." Sam said, "we gave bonuses across the board last Xmas, but in June, we'll be giving bonuses again but this time they will be based on longevity, productivity, and positions of essential responsibility and leadership, as with foremen. We plan to take care of our workers—if you get my drift."

Changing the subject, Ike wanted to share some news. "I've been talking to several Colorado Colt salesmen. The reality is that Colt and other gun manufacturers are developing a semi-automatic pistol. From now on the revolver will be a handgun with a revolving cylinder and the pistol will now refer to this new handgun. This will be a revolution in handguns that will hold for a century. The way this will affect you will be because of the new cartridge caliber this pistol will use—the 45ACP."

"Ah, yes. Alden Picket, the Colt district sales director has mentioned this as an upcoming event." "Hu-um, my old boss is not to be trusted. You see, Colt will win the military contract with their automatic pistol in 45ACP—but Colt makes guns, not ammunition. Now how can you expect the salesmen to sell a new handgun if there is no ammo on the market. Watch out for Mister Picket, he doesn't have your business in the forefront, he's trying to make a buck off you. He's going to try to get you to make the 45 casings and load them. Then he'll fenagle a way to buy them off you at a discount." "You're correct, he already gave us a 5-man drawing die in 45ACP with the not-so-subtle suggestion."

"So, as it stands, the ammo will come from Winchester and Remington-UMC (Union Metallic Cartridge). That means, it will take years to saturate the eastern market before the ammo will ever cross the Mississippi River. So, the only way Colt will sell these new pistols out West is if the private sector makes the casings and loads the ammo—AND THAT MEANS YOU c/o TEXAS LOAD."

Amy was a bit surprised as she said, "that was very clear, we'll heed your warning and start preparing. What do you think we should specifically do, knowing we'll be busy with your orders?"

"Right now, I agree, you'll be very busy keeping up with orders. Later, your BP press will be your best income producer, and eventually the ammo production of smokeless ammo will also go down once your presses sell for loading smokeless ammo with the new accessories you're holding back (scale, powder, and priming system). So, the question will be how fast this rolling evolution will occur, so you need to be ready." "Such as how?"

"It depends on what have you done so far?" Sam answered, "our #5 five-man brass cartridge fabricator will be installed in two weeks. We've also purchase #2 and #3-45ACP complete sets of drawing dies." "Good start, now add:

1. Order machine #6 in 45ACP and order two more drawing dies in 45ACP—that will make five sets for production and one as a spare, or for the last machine if put in use. Why? Because Big Blue won't be able to provide the machines and dies that this 45ACP madness will cause. Time to order is now when the demand is low.

2. Start building a large inventory of 230 grain Round Nose hardcast lead bullets sized .451 inch.

3. Increase your medium burn rate powder inventory to handle the heavy bullet weight.,

4. Correspondingly, build your large pistol primers to match the bullets and powder."

"I cannot emphasize enough the rush that will occur once the gun lovers get their eyes and hands on a semi-automatic pistol. I suspect this could take your business into retirement. My sources say, that the change will happen so suddenly, that very few companies will be ready. You can be ready, and get ahead of the pack."

Sam and Amy were quiet and pensive, as Amy gave Sam the nod.

Sam said, "I've always said that 'a word to the wise should be adequate,' and we will be ready—I assure you. Plus, our getting geared up for this revolution will also guarantee your job as our salesman for several more years, heh?" "Yes Sir, also likely into my retirement—I admit it."

Ike continued, "by tradition, I always save the more complicated issues for last. As you noticed, I had one Saturday meeting. This was a busy but pleasant owner of three large gun shops in the city that catered to the four speed shooting clubs. This man went crazy when I offered unlimited smokeless ammo. So he ordered:

TEN—Package A in 38 Target (960 fifty round boxes) = $2,400
TWO—Package A in 38 Hot (192 fifty round boxes) = $480
TWO—Package B in 44 Hot (128 fifty round boxes) = $384
THREE—Presses with accessory kits = $165
Total = $3,429

Sam had uplifting eyebrows as he said, "that's an incredible order. Why is it complicated?" "For two reasons, the first being that his name is Ivan Crandall." "Whoa, I guess he never got to Canada as planned. What happened?" "He told me that when he got to Denver there was a big estate auction of three gun shops. He went to the auction and started bidding. To his surprise, he won the bid for $900, and the rest is history."

Amy looked at Sam who simply shrugged his shoulder. "There is no animosity here, so his money is as good as anyone else—actually I'm glad he has done well for himself. What is the other complicated issue?" Well, Mister Crandall has a contract with

Colt for 100 of their new Colt automatic pistols. These are promised to the four speed shooting clubs, but as you know, a new gun without ammo doesn't fly. So, Mister Crandall made this request. He wants 10 boxes of loaded 45ACP ammo for every pistol he sells—and will take them anytime you load them. That means he wants 1,000 boxes of 50 round each. I quoted the high price of $4 a box and he laughed as he wrote this bank draft for $4,000 and this separate draft for $3,429 for the other ammo—but he said one was tied to the other, meaning you accept both or no deal?"

Sam was not believing what the offer was, as he added, "but Ike you overcharged him for the 45ACP ammo." "Could be, but Crandall didn't think so. Besides, by the time you get into the market, the ammo will be worth $4 a box." Amy saw a smile on Sam's face and as soon as he added a nod, she grabbed the two drafts and said, "nice job Mister Webb. Now I know why you sold so much ammo. You are a diplomatic magician. Your bonus will reflect our ultra-satisfaction and Thank You, see you in two weeks."

***

CHAPTER 4

Day to Day and Beyond

Things had been going well but extremely busy trying to stay ahead of the Denver orders. It was now the Thursday payday and tomorrow would be the foreman's biweekly meeting that now had been changed to the morning after each payday. The Duo was contemplating the ever-ongoing dilemma as to whether more loaders were needed. It was Amy that finally had an answer that made sense.

"Sam, I finally have enough figures that allows us to plan the future. Follow my statistics: 2,000 rounds per loader X 30 loaders = 60,000 rounds per day or 300,000 per week. So let's work with the weekly 300,000 rounds—that comes to 6,000 fifty-round boxes OR 250 fifty-pound fixed rate boxes ÷ 6 = 41 300-pound crates.

"Now multiply everything by 52 weeks a year and you come to a whopping 15.6 million rounds a year or 312,000 fifty round boxes a year. Multiply 312,000 boxes by our current $2.50 for 38's and that comes to another whopping $780,000." "To simplify matters, you can read the ledger later on, but suffice it to say that I have computed the expenses for 30 loaders at $5 a day and labor comes to $39,000, cost of goods at the same $1.80 per 50 round box comes to $561,000. I've also added an inflated amount of $100,000 for depreciation, overhead and misc. expenses. Yet, we are still making $80,000 a year in profit for loading ammo, plus the uncounted income from selling casings to Winchester and the sale of your presses and accessories."

"Now I prepared all this to point out that we are big enough, and sometimes there is no advantage to grow beyond our marketable product. Yes, right now there is a flood of orders coming in, but like any flood, the waters will recede and with too many loaders, we'll have to lay some off. I truly believe that we'll plateau with our orders and 30 loaders is enough. I agree that we would benefit from having a few extra loaders on board because we'll lose with sick days, workers on personal days, ladies with bad monthly cycles, pregnant gals that can't put in a full day, and even moms on maternity leave." "Ok, it makes sense, we'll add 4 more loaders and save two machines for you and me, incase it's needed. So we'll make four rows of 9 benches/loaders. So what do we do with the extra 8 feet of space?" "Wait and I think Irene will tell you what to do with that, heh."

Sam then added, "to prepare for the meeting, I think it's time to discuss what Alden Pickett and Ike mentioned about the new 45ACP cartridge, and what we are prepared to do about it." "Ok, let's make a list and we'll discuss it tomorrow."

As the foremen were getting their teams started for the day, the Duo was busy reading a letter that came in yesterday, but they had not had the time to even open the envelope. At 9AM, Sam called the meeting to order. "I would like to start by discussing an issue that has come to our attention by Alden Pickett, Colt District Sales for this Texas northern area, and by Ike Webb from the Colorado Colt salesmen."

Sam and Amy went thru a detailed explanation of the new Colt handgun called a semi-automatic pistol that will revolutionize the handgun industry—and with a new cartridge called 45ACP. To summarize, Sam said, "of specific interest is the fact that Colt builds guns but does not manufacture ammo. It was the consensus of Pickett and Webb that ammo would not cross the Mississippi for a year or more, and without ammo, Colt wouldn't be selling pistols out West. It would be up to companies like ours to make the new cartridge and load it for sale—to the Texas and Colorado gun shops, and possibly to other states—not to sell the loaded ammo to Colt at a discount."

At that point, Amy distributed to all present, a new casing for the 45ACP. Glen had already studied this case and was asked to describe its unique features. "This case is shorter than the 44 special and weighs 12 pounds per 1,000 casings compared to 13 pounds per thousand for 44 special. It takes a 230 RN bullet, with a diameter of .451 inch, which is smaller than the 45 Long Colt at .452 inch. The body has a slight taper like the 30-30 casings. The new case is different from our revolver ammo in that it is rimless. That is a misnomer because there is a rim, but it is rebated and is not wider than the body of the case. In addition, the rebated rim is also undercut to form an extraction groove. And for you Ann, it takes a large pistol primer and loads best with the medium burn rate we are presently using—at 6.5 grains to achieve a velocity of 850 fps, or 7.0 grains for a velocity of 900fps. The big issue is that it uses a taper crimp to remove the belled casing, but not to be crimped like the revolver roll crimps—in other words the taper crimp is to only remove the belling because the case headspaces on the case mouth—not on the rim as with revolver ammo."

Amy then took over. "On this subject, yesterday we received a letter from Ira Winchester, and I would like to read it to you in its entirety."

> *Dear Sam and Amy,*
>
> *As you know by now, we will soon have a revolutionary new semi-automatic Colt pistol come on the market. The big issue for both Winchester and TEXAS LOAD is that this pistol comes with a new cartridge, 45ACP. Since Colt does not make ammo, that is why I am writing this letter.*
>
> *You currently have a year left on our 2-year arrangement. You have been regular in sending Winchester a monthly 300-pound crate of 30-30 casings—but we have finally caught*

up on the supply and demand for this cartridge. For this reason I now have a new proposal. We are prepared to add one more year to the contract if you agree to send us a 300-pound crate of 45ACP each month. In return, we will pay you 11 cents per casing like we did with the 30-30 casings, plus we will increase your discounted price of 10% to 20% for unlimited primers with free shipping to you—effective immediately upon your signing this contract.

It is clear that we need to start building an inventory for this casing, and we need to tool up to make them. Getting casings from you is crucial for us since it will be six months before we even can start making them. In addition to my proposal, I will personally contact Dupont Powder and Missouri Lead to notify them that Winchester is in a contractual agreement with TEXAS LOAD. As our partner in providing us with casings, we will expect these two providers to deal with TEXAS LOAD as if they are dealing with Winchester. I am certain that these two companies will look at my request as a friendly reminder and not a threat.

In closing, I hope we can continue our working status, and extend our contract another two years. If you sign the contract, send it by postal service, but notify me by telegram so I can start the paperwork at my end and not delay your discount. Respectfully, Ira Winchester

There was total silence in the office as Neil was the first to speak. "Goodness gracious, what a deal!" Every foreman spoke in favor of the deal as Amy said, "we agree and have already signed it." Sam then took over. "Ok, now how to make this all happen. Irene, here is your sequence of needed events:

1. Mail the contract and notify Ira, by telegram, that we have signed it, and will be sending his first shipment as soon as we can gear up.

2. Contact Big Blue. They have the #5 five-man machine arriving nest week. Notify them that you want to change the caliber to 45ACP.

3. Also with Big Blue, order the #6 machine also in 45ACP.

4. Again with Big Blue, order an extra 38 full set die and an extra 45ACP full set drawing die as well—as spares.

5. Notify Lionel Lofton that we need 24 complete loading 4-die sets for 45ACP—that will perk up his eyebrows.

6. Start building a separate inventory of loading components for this new cartridge—to include the separate brass buds. For now, use the abandoned steel storage room for these separate components. That means that any bullets already in that storage room will need to be moved to the back of A-Wing."

"Glen, your next. As soon as the #5 machine is installed with the 45ACP dies, you're moving back to brass fabrication. Take 4 men from the other machines and get trained by the Big Blue technician. Start making your first order of 45ACP cases. It takes 25,000 casings to weigh 300 pounds and you should be able to do this order in five days.

Afterwards, it all depends on what the need is, and I'll be working with you and Elton to make a decision. It is clear that the #5 machine will stay set up for 45ACP, but the #6 machine can be set up for whatever we need. I may add that for now, our main directive is to supply the 38 and 44 cases that the loaders need, and supplying Winchester with our contractual commitment—everything else is building an elective future inventory."

"Now Neil, how are things going with building presses?" "We have built 50 presses and they are all boxed up and stored in the processing room. It's going to take another 4 weeks to finish the other 50, now that we'll be losing Glen. Irene is keeping our alloys well supplied and all the machines are working well. The ventilation fans are keeping the air fresh and that was a nice touch to install them. So, we're good, and when the three college boys arrive, we'll be able to send Elmer and Paul back to brass fabrication. Finally, I take it that we'll be building press accessory parts for the foreseeable future, heh?" "Yes."

"Elton, you're next." "In view of this coming new cartridge, staffing will become crucial and we need to plan ahead. Currently, I have 17 fabricators working, plus me and Glen, and Elmer and Paul coming back. With the four college boys, that will make a staff of 25 men. Any idea how we're going to staff the #6 machine?" "Hu-um, that's a well taken and very good question. Amy and I will be working on this ASAP." "Great, now I have a dilemma, I have a man who is not working up to par and is very exhausted come 5 o'clock." "Is that Hans?" "Yes." "Well look outside the office, look at who is working with Lucille. I suspect the problem is about to be resolved and will get back to you." "Ok, and finally, now that Glen will be coming back, who will be the foreman, Glen or me?" The Duo looked at each other and paused. When Amy shrugged her shoulders, Sam said, "you are Elton. Glen, Elmer and Paul will have the same salary as a foreman. but will be classified as the official floaters from machining to fabrication." "Boy that was what is called 'thinking on your feet,' heh. Again you show the wisdom of Solomon and that's a great virtue and asset in a boss. Glen, are you satisfied with that?" "Absolutely." "Well, so am I."

"Luke step right up." "I don't have a single issue. Kent is a life saver, and everything is running smooth. I have some free time each day to help out at the processing table. I may add that I have purchased a new 300-pound loader that now runs on a battery that we keep charged with a battery charger. The nice thing is that it can lift a 300-pound railroad crate and stack them three crates high. More on this later."

"Ida, you're next." "Amy is now off the processing tables. She has her own section and is busy 100% of the time. We get some intermittent help from Irene and Luke, but I suspect that with Ike working in Colorado that we're going to need some more regular parttime help." Amy said, "Mom turn around, look at who is working with Aunt Lucille right now." "Oh my, that would be perfect. He's a pleasant and fast worker."

"Ann, what is new with the loaders. "Well, I just had my first 'no show' without it scheduled or even a morning phone call. How do you want me to deal with that?" "I may be wrong, but Cyrus has never come to the shop unless there is a problem. I suspect the answer is there, so I'll get back to you on that."

"Ok, well things are going very well. In view of the extra orders, am I planning to stay with 30 loaders as I now have, or what are your plans?" Amy answered, "right now, I feel like I'm standing in a dry gulch with a flash flood coming at me, but eventually the flood waters will recede. Sam and I have decided that we are as big as we want to get, and eventually the orders will plateau. Yet we like the production afforded by 30 loaders. So we've decided to add four more loaders to compensate for sick days, personal days, pregnant gals cutting down their hours, and weeks of maternity leave. So we'll rearrange the rows to have four rows of nine benches with two benches for me and Amy if the need arises. Your two benches will continue to be perpendicular to the four rows."

Sam was about to conclude the meeting when he asked if anyone had an idea of what to do with the extra 8 feet from a bench being removed. There was a persistent silence that led Sam to prepare to close the meeting when Irene exploded with an off the cuff statement. "PUNCH A HOLE IN THE WALL, ADD AN 8-FOOT ARCHWAY, AND BUILD A WAREHOUSE."

*

Amy looked at Sam and whispered, "I suspected this was coming, since Irene has been desperate to find places to store supplies. Hear her out, heh." "Well Irene, tell me why we would ever consider another construction project since we just added 6,000 square feet." "I know, but that was production space with the minimal storage space. Right now all of our storage spaces are full except the back of A-Wing and the old steel room. I will fill the steel room with 45ACP components, but where do I put the casings you wish for us to start hoarding. Bottom line, we have two rail cars arriving this coming week, and I have no idea where to put the supplies. Since the old loading/receiving area is full to the ceiling, I guess we'll have to dismantle those extra six loading benches and use the space for storage, while turning the floor area into a packed can of sardines. I'm sorry to be so verbal, but for now, I am holding ordering any supplies till we make room. Actually, we have enough storage to just replace what we use up on a weekly basis, and there is no way to build an inventory for the future. If that is what you want, we can do it—but I thought you wanted me to build inventories for anticipating the future demands?"

Sam looked at Amy as she again whispered, "we have plenty of money, so why not build a warehouse. The time to build inventories is when we have good income, and the components are available."

Sam looked at Irene and said, "how big a warehouse do you want and with or without shelves."

"40 X 125 feet with posts just like B-Wing, a wide

center aisle for Luke's electric lift, an open area on the left for stacking crates three high, and sideway shelves on the right side. Ventilation fans to control humidity, plenty of lights, bars in the windows, and a locked door in the archway."

"You got it, I'll go see Bert today and suspect we'll be moving in within three weeks. Till then, our foremen will reorganize their area to make room for your supplies, and please do not cancel your orders. We will all manage till the warehouse is ready. Nice job Irene."

"Anything else?" "Amy lifted her hand, "Sorry but I forgot to mention that we had a surprise visit from Lloyds of London. He liked what he saw and approved our liability protection application for our loaded ammo and for the sale of the BP loading presses. He especially liked the signed release of liability from the gun shops. The premium cost is a bit pricey at $3,000 a year, but if we add bars in our windows the price will go down to $2,500 and if we add armed nightwatchmen, the price will again drop to $2,000." "Something for us to discuss at a later time. And so, that brings this meeting to a close, but I must say it was a great meeting. Many of these issues will be followed up in two weeks."

With the foremen back to their work site, Sam welcomed Hans to come in as he told Cyrus that he was next. "Well Hans, what can I do for you?" "Well, things are changing. I can't put out my quota, I'm down to 750 casings a day, and slowing down the other workers. I get home so exhausted that I fall asleep before dinner, can't enjoy dinner, and go to bed right after dinner. To make it worse, I wake up exhausted before I get to work. I guess my age of 67 is getting to me."

"I can understand that, but what do you want to do? Do you want to retire or take an easier and parttime job." "Would you allow me to come to work at the processing tables, during the 10AM break, and leave at the 2:45PM break. If that doesn't work out, I will retire." "Of course, and you might as well start today, heh?" "Why not, I've already been at it an hour already. Ha, ha, ha-ah!"

"Cyrus, please come in. What do you need?" "I need for you and Miss Amy to come to my apartment. Esmerelda Layton has been severely beaten." "Let me get Amy and we'll follow you." Walking into the barn, the Duo went into Cyrus's apartment. When they saw their friend's black eye, Amy took her in her arms and tried to console her. "I'm sorry Miss Amy, I didn't want you to see me like this, and I just couldn't go in the shop like this." Amy must have been squeezing too hard as Esmerelda winced in pain. Amy asked, "Can I see your back?" Esmeralda continued to cry as she lifted her blouse. "Oh my God, you're covered in bruises, is the front the same?" "Yes." "You may have some fractured ribs; Cyrus would you go get Doc Kipp?" "Yes Miss Amy, on my way."

While they were waiting for the Doc, Amy convinced Esmerelda to tell them what was going on. "I've been living with this man for one year. He used to work for the freight office, but two months ago he lost his job because he was drinking on the job. For two months, he's done nothing but drinking. He takes my pay as soon as I come home. He's supposed to pay my mortgage and the credit at Asa's store, but he hasn't done it. He just drinks my wages away. Every time I confront him, he beats me and performs relations on me in my, uh-uh intestine. Last night, I decided to fight back but the beating I got knocked me senseless, and then he again performed those carnal relations on me. I must have passed out since I woke this morning covered with bruises and a real black 'shiner.' I left the house while he was still sleeping off a wild drinking night. I'm afraid to go back to my house, because everything will continue, if he doesn't kill me, for when he drinks, he turns into a violent animal. He's a dangerous man who loves to fistfight and has a killer righthand punch."

As Doc Kipp was arriving, Sam asked, "what's this man's name, where do you live, and do you have a gun?" "Efrain Bull, I live at 12 Elm Street, and I use to have my own 'single shot shotgun,' but he sold it weeks ago for whiskey." As Doc Kipp went in to examine Esmerelda, the Duo stepped out.

Doc Kipp stepped out and said, "that's a sad situation. She is covered with bruises, and a couple of cracked but undisplaced ribs. She also has internal tears, but all will heal. What can we do about this beast that would do this to a woman?" Sam added, "not to worry Doc, we will cure him of his paraphiliac behavior, and he'll be heading permanently out of town today."

As Doc Kipp was leaving, he suggested she needed some breakfast. Amy then asked Cyrus, "would you stay with her and make her some coffee and breakfast, we have to fix this problem permanently, and we'll return afterwards." "Of course, be happy to."

The Duo walked to the nearby Elm Street as Amy asked how they were going to cure this man of his perverted paraphiliac tendency. Sam stopped and picked up two four-inch rocks off the street. "This should do it. Now let me disable his right arm first, then you take the lead and do what you feel will be a decisive deterrent to ever come back to this town. You have to be firm, because a threat from a woman is often disregarded."

Arriving at 12 Elm, Sam applied a loud knock and waited. Eventually a scruffy ill-kept man appeared at the door and said, "what in hell do you want and who are you?" "I am the messenger to deliver $100 to a lucky man, let me shake your hand." Efrain naturally extended his hand as it could be tied to $100. Sam grabbed his hand, moved behind him, as he pulled his right hand behind his back until the shoulder popped out. Things happened so fast that Efrain had a delayed scream as he turned white as a sheet. Amy then stepped forward and popped him on the forehead with her sap. Mister Bull dropped to his knees.

Sam quickly stood him back up, and pulled down his pants. Amy lifted the 4-pound rocks and pancaked them onto his oysters. The impact was electrifying as Efrain saw the rock come down on the other rock again and smash the oysters to mush. Efrain kept cradling his sac with his left hand and yelling the sound of a white man being scalped. Amy said, "well Mister Bull, I'd say you'll never be able to put your 'pa-ding' in any woman's rectum ever again, actually the only hole you'll ever use is the hole in the privy—ha, ha, ha-ah."

Efrain was foaming around his lips as well as spitting away. Amy said, "are you paying attention to me?" Without a response, she reached in his back and grabbed his right index finger and twisted it till it snapped several times. Efrain was again yelling away and not paying attention when Amy stuck a long fingernail into one of his eyes. Efrain started arching up and down as in a convulsion. It was then that Sam said, "I don't think Mister Bull still believes your intentions." "Well this will work."

Amy applied pressure to his trachea just below the Adam's apple. Efrain started thrashing about, turned blue, eyes bugged out, tongue protruding and turning blue. Just before he lost consciousness, she let off the pressure as Efrain gasped and slowly regained his color. "Gee, that was fun, let's do it again and this time I'll let you die—ha, ha, ha-ah." The pressure went back on and everything was repeated as Sam began to wonder if Amy really meant to kill him. Just as his heart was about to stop, she let off the pressure and the gasping restarted.

Sam looked at Efrain and said, "do you now believe that if you ever return to town, that we will kill you?" "Yes Sir, I'll leave by train today and you'll never see me again." Amy leaned onto his face and said, "I hope you change your mind and come back, because I REALLY WANT TO KILL YOU BY CUTTING OFF YOUR PA-DING—HA, HA, HA-AH."

The Duo finally got him moving and packed a carpet bag of his clothing and personal items. He had $48 in his pocket, Esmerelda's salary minus a bottle of whiskey. It took a while to get him walking because of the grapefruit mass in his crotch, but when he was able to move about, Sam lifted the dislocated shoulder's arm up and popped the ball back in its socket. Sam then said, "I'll bring him to the train depot and make sure he gets on the train. Meanwhile, go to Asa's and select enough vittles for a week to 10 days, plus a single shot shotgun with a box of OO Buckshot, and pay off her credit and leave another $100 on the book. Leave everything there for Cyrus to pick up. Then go to the bank, pay off Ike's and Esmerelda's mortgages, then we'll meet at the train depot."

It took another hour for the Duo to witness Efrain boarding the train to Oklahoma City. Seeing him in the passenger window, they waited for the train to depart before returning to Cyrus's apartment. "Esmerelda, Mister Bull is gone forever, Cyrus will take you home. You are now on short term disability till your bruises and ribs heal, and your shiner clears. Cyrus will bring you the vittles we chose at Asa's, and will check on you in two days, and then once a week to pick up what you need. Here is $100 which is your four week's pay. Your mortgage has been paid off, as a gift to you, as a valued employee. We are looking forward to seeing you back at work. Oh, and by the way, Mister Bull was also permanently cured of his perverted carnal ways—the hard way."

Back at work, Amy told Ann that Esmeralda was on short term disability for one month. Meanwhile, Sam went to see Bert Holiday in regard to a warehouse.

***

CHAPTER 5

In Full Swing

Sam walked into Bert Holiday's construction company that same day. "Hello Bert, well it looks like we need some more construction." "What do you need, more production area?" "No, I think with three production sections in two wings, that we're all set there. What we need is more storage so we can build an inventory of supplies during the good times. So we need a warehouse." "Well, let's go over the specifics."

"Ok, pop a hole in the wall in A-Wing and build an 8-foot archway with locking double doors. Add a warehouse 40 feet wide by 125 feet long with the same post system as in B-Wing. Leave the left side of the warehouse open to stack crates, and the right side with free-standing shelves perpendicular to the wide aisle. Finish the walls with plywood, add three rows of ceiling lights with the center one over the aisle, a dozen outlets on the walls, and ceiling fans for ventilation and humidity control. New this time, iron bars in the windows. Again, the same brick walls and concrete floor. What did I forget?" "Very little, except we'll need a separate entrance electrical box since your two other electrical systems are loaded enough. For humidity control, we'll add a separate kerosene furnace for hot air in the winter and air circulation in the summer by using the furnace fans."

In addition, we'd like you to add iron bars on A and B Wings. We are adding security watchmen, and the insurance premiums are significantly reduced with these two changes. Plus, this security change requires an outside light on every wall or every 50 feet for long walls—and on a separate circuit. And since we'll have our security men spend time inside and outside, we need two inside lights for each wing plus one over the processing tables and one in the office—on separate circuits so we can pull the fuse boxes for every other circuit when we close up shop."

"Great, we'll start digging the footing today and pour concrete in the morning." "Here is a deposit of $5,000 to get started, and see any foreman to find out where the archway will be." "So basically, this is a shorten version of B-Wing without storage rooms or double phase power, but with triple decker shelving on half the room." "Yes Sir. How long to build?" "Two weeks minimum—three weeks maximum!"

His next stop was the Star Security Agency. Sam found out that the staff were all trained and were armed with a revolver and a pump shotgun. The owner, Dale Hicks, explained that they had 30 customers in town and Sam was given their names as references. Sam liked what he heard and made arrangements to hire the agency. He would have a man 5PM to Midnight, and another from Midnight to 7AM—seven days a week. Dale explained that the team would be rotated each week as they were with other customers—a system that was proven the most efficient. To Sam's surprise, if any watchman had a problem, he could take the phone and call the shift supervisor's team for assistance. The cost was $5 per shift and with 14 shifts a week, his cost would be $70 a week but without any benefits, vacation days or bonuses.

His next stop was the telegraph office where he decided to send a request to Big Blu. His telegram read:

FROM TEXAS LOAD C/O SAM BALINGER DALLAS TX

IN NEED OF BRASS FABRICATORS STOP

ANY KNOWN TRAINED WORKERS AVAILABLE STOP

WOULD GLADLY ACCEPT RECENT GRADUATES STOP

OFFERING LIVING WAGE PLUS BENEFITS STOP

NEED SIX WORKERS TO FILL MY SHOP STOP

WILL PAY TRANSPORTATION, HOUSING AND MEALS

FOR A THREE DAY INTERVIEW STOP

As Sam was about to leave, the telegrapher stopped him. "Sir, you are getting an answer live. It says in rare and expensive letter form: From Jim at Big Blue. I know who you are, know your wage offers and benefits from my technicians that have been in your shop. We sponsor a trade college in El Paso that has an eight-month class graduating June 1. These graduates are well trained, but the market for their trade in Arizona and California is saturated. I can find six that, have no local family ties, and would be willing to move to Dallas. I can send them to you next week and you can refund their train ticket. Let me know by tomorrow morning. Jim at Big Blue.

The telegrapher looked at Sam as he said, "send this message back. Send them next week on Thursday and they will return Sunday. Thank You, Sam Balinger." "Sure, that will be 30 cents for 15 words." Jim's answer was three words. "Done, good choice."

Sam was walking back to the shop when he saw a sign that read, "Rosie's Cleaning Service." Sam thought he would mention it to Amy. As he arrived in the shop, it seemed like total mayhem at the processing tables. Hans, Ida, and Lucille could not keep up with the ammo production and clearly needed help. Sam jumped in and stayed at the job till Irene and Luke showed up after the last break of the day.

That evening, they decided that a cleaning service was overdue and would send Irene to negotiate a thorough cleaning on Saturday and two short cleanings on Tuesday and Thursday evenings. Also, to manage the flood of extra-large orders from Colorado, the Duo decided to hire one of the loaders wives, a victim of the "empty nest syndrome." Her name was Edna Griffin, and an old friend of Ida's. This freed up Sam to work on the soon to visit college boys from El Paso, the Houston college boys arriving in May, interviewing for four more loaders, and watching the construction along.

After a week, the walls were already halfway up at 5 feet and the trusses were being built. The framing for the inside wall with its insulation board and vapor barrier were also going up. Done at the end of the second week were, the inside wall framing, the trusses, the steel roof, the brick walls, and the entrance arch with double doors. A double door, at the end of the warehouse, was added for wagon freight direct deliveries. The remainder of the supplies came from the railroad at the new loading/receiving area. The third week would be for finishing the ceiling and walls, insulating the ceilings, adding ventilation fans and ductwork, adding a furnace and ductwork, and new wiring for lights and outlets. While this was being done, another team at the shop was building the free-standing triple decker shelves. Bert was certain that the supplies could be moved in during the third week's weekend.

*

Since the warehouse would be finished this weekend, Sam notified Jim at Big Blue to change the college boy's visit to next weekend. This weekend would be dedicated to the big move to C-Wing. All week, Sam met with Bert twice a day to clarify some finishing touches.

1. Do not paint the floor for one year. Moisture has to escape the concrete to avoid paint lifting.
2. Luke got involved with the shelves. He wanted two 3 X 8 -foot shelves with a 4-foot-wide aisle between two shelves—and five of these double back-to-back shelves to cover only 50 lineal feet. At the end of each shelf aisle would be a wall outlet and a light over the center of the aisle. The shelves would be 2 feet apart and three high. Bert added that free standing shelves needed to be reinforced

with half inch plywood at each end and a full backing of half inch plywood in the back. The framing would be of 2X6 lumber. The fourth top shelf would be left open for holding sheets of ammo boxes that did not fit under the processing tables.

3. Luke also chose where to put the other outlets—at both ends of the warehouse and a battery of them centrally located on the open left side.

4. A roof and deck was added outside the double doors to store the empty railroad crates.

5. A supply of 4X4 inch lumber by 36 inch was needed to keep the crates off the concrete floor, and also served to separate each crate so the hydraulic lifting blades could fit under the crates.

6. A portable grinding machine would be moved to the back porch to grind up cardboard boxes into chips that were bagged and sold to chicken and pig farms as bedding—50 cents per 50-pound bag.

7. Every truss supporting post had attached: a set of pliers, a hammer, and two sizes of crow bars to open up the railroad crates—plus a bucket to hold the used nails.

Bert was surprised at only having 10 double ended shelves to cover 50 feet by 8 feet. Luke's answer was that if we were rushed, the shelf items of powder, primers, oil, and brass cleaning agents would stay in railroad crates till they were needed. He even dared say, "if the shelves prove to be too much work to keep items on the shelves, that they would be dismantled and thrown out. Then the warehouse would be for railroad crates and other boxed supplies.

During that last week, Sam found himself busy plugging in some extra help in loading, brass fabrication, and even milling some parts. It was nice to see the processing tables well manned and he even saw Irene one day move over to Amy's table. All week, the railroad sent a boxcar to load the finalized orders, and thereby keeping the loading area emptied at least once a day.

Friday finally came, and Bert was picking up and cleaning the warehouse. Sam went around with Luke and Irene to get a tally of what needed to be moved. At lunch time, Sam announced that he needed men to help with the move of heavy boxes, and would pay time and a half. In no time he ended up with a dozen men who volunteered.

Saturday arrived. The Duo had picked up several pastries and had coffee ready. Sam conducted the meeting. Luke will direct, according to his master plan, where everything goes. Irene will choose which storage room to empty in proper sequence, Kent would pick up a 300-pound crate and bring it to Luke's chosen spot. This continued for two solid hours when the first break arrived.

During the break, the railroad men arrived with two full boxcars of supplies—all in crates. Sam made a deal with the workers who were to unload the crates and leave them in the loading area. For 50 cents a crate, the workers would wheel every crate into the warehouse and stack them where Luke directed.

After the break, with the steel room empty of brass buds, Neil moved the old steel racks to the present room in B-Wing and set the racks up. During the day, the workers moved all the powder to the bottom shelves where the air was cooler, the primers to the second shelf, and the oils and cleaning solutions to the third top shelf. Once the shelves were all full, everything left over was stored in crates and placed in their own rows for easy access.

By 3PM, the A-Wing storage room next to the lunchroom was empty, the old steel room empty, and the lead bullets for 38s and 44s left stacked at the end of A-Wing as before. B-Wing storage room was also emptied and would become a storage room for the completed presses waiting for shipping. At this point, the old steel room and the storage room next to the lunchroom would stay empty till a need came up.

The two railroad workers had moved 40 crates, and were happy to go home with an extra $20 between the two of them. At the end of the day, the 10 shelves were fully loaded and with tied bundles of different boxes on the top shelves. About half of the remaining open square footage was left unused. All 45ACP components had been placed at the far end of the shelf side—being stored there in crates, away from other supplies, till ready to be used.

By 4PM, everyone was heading home. The Duo stayed to meet the first nightwatchman, and to review what his duties would entail—although it was suspected that he had been properly guided before he got to work. The only directive that the watchman had not been told was that all power was to be off, for fire security, by pulling the many fuse boxes, except for the one fuse box that controlled the security lights inside and outside. That meant, visiting the electrical room in each wing. Also to avoid flood damage from busted water lines, once there was no security during weekend days, the main water valve was to be shut off.

So the Duo finally got home in time to bathe and change for an evening of dining and dancing with their friends. Finally, Sunday was truly a lounging day. The Duo stayed in their sleepwear till noon when there was a knock at the door. Sam opened the door to find Winston Hutchins, master director of the local speed shooting club. "Well, come in, I haven't seen you for some time. What brings you here today?" "I need to show you something very important. Will you join me at the range, it will only take a half hour of your time." "Sure, have a seat and we'll get dressed."

Arriving at the range, Winston took out a satchel and pulled out a strange looking firearm. "Alden Picket lent me this prototype; it is Colt's new semi-automatic pistol. All my team members have fired a 7-round magazine, and I have four magazines for both of you to try. Let me show you how to load it and remove the safety." Sam was shown two cardboard targets and told to shoot a 7-round magazine at each target, as fast as he could pull the trigger, eject the spent magazine, and shoot off the other loaded magazine at the other target.

Sam, once loaded, started firing—bang-bang-bang-bang-bang-bang-bang. He ejected the magazine, inserted the other one and repeated the 7-shot string. "Mercy, this is almost frightening. There is no doubt that this will bring an end to the revolver era which has been king for a hundred years." Winston added, "now look at the targets, each bullet hole is 2 inch higher on the target than the last one. That's because you fired the next round before the pistol had returned from its lifting recoil. Had you fired faster, it would have had a 3-or 4-inch spread. Ok Amy, it's your turn. Let me put up some new targets, and then let fly."

Amy was psyched and pushed the envelope. After all 14 rounds, the targets showed a 1 inch spread because she shot a bit slower. Sam then asked, "that was an amazing demo, but for what purpose?" "Well, I ordered and paid for 25 of these pistols at $50 each with three magazines. I also ordered and prepaid 25 speed holsters with two magazine holders. The only problem is that there is no ammo to be found, and my team wants to start shooting this automatic, and put up their 1898 revolvers."

"Hu-um, I see. I suppose you want to reserve some loaded ammo once we start loading this new caliber, heh?" "Yes, actually I would like to prepay for my order!" "How many boxes?" "Each man wants 10 boxes of 50-round count." "That's 250 boxes at $4 each, or $1,000." "Actually, I have $1500 left over, so could I pay for 375 boxes?" "Sure, because Amy and I will likely join you, heh, but future orders must come from the local gun shops once the market demand is supplied." "Here is your $1500 bank draft. Now give me $140 and I'll include two more pistols with the magazines, holsters and magazine holders." "Ok, that way, I'll guarantee the ammo the day you hand me my two pistols."

Getting back home, the Duo was in a quandary. Amy asked, "have we already started to build the brass casing inventory?" "Yes, Glen has kept those four men working #5 machine and is producing 25,000 casings a week. We've sent one batch to Winchester and we're on track to producing 25,000 casings a month for Winchester at $2,500, and 75,000 casings monthly for building our own inventory. We haven't decided what to do with machine #6 yet, but we also don't have the manpower till the Houston college boys arrive and or we convince the El Paso group to move and join our family. I can guarantee you that Irene is building a nice surplus of powder, primers, brass buds, and bullets for the new cartridge—45ACP."

"So, the only decision is when do we start loading 45ACP cartridges." "Well, a lot depends on how many orders we continue to get for 38s and 44s, as well as when the Colt pistols will appear in gun shops. So, I think I'll send a telegram to Alden Pickett and ask for some 'head's up' information. For now, we'll have a busy week handling the persistent flood of orders and we have to get ready to entertain those boys from El Paso. Plus tomorrow I have those interviews to fill out those four spots."

*

This time Irene had conducted the preliminary physical test and the elimination set of work conditions. She had reduced it to four applicants, again all 18-year-old women with a high school degree. Sam and Amy then met with each applicant. They collected names, addresses, phone numbers, nearest of kin and so on. During the interviews two crucial facts became known. These gals, like many of the previous ones, wanted the job for the same reasons—independence with a living wage and benefits, and the opportunity to work with young single men. All four gals were hired, and training would start in the morning. After the gals left, Amy pointed out, "you know this drive to meet a partner is good for our company. Our workers are much more motivated when a second person is involved in their lives."

A few days later, the hotel rooms for all six college boys from El Paso were set along with paid up meals. To Sam's surprise, Alden Pickett showed up that Wednesday. "Hello Sam, I got your telegram and decided to come visit you. I heard you liked Colt's pistol and you promised Winston some 375 boxes of 45ACP ammo." "Yes, that's the second order I take. The other was from a Denver gun shop. I only plan to take prepaid gun shop orders, but I took Winston's order because Amy and I belong to that shooting club."

"Well, Colt will have pistols for delivery to Texas gun shops about May of next year." "In that case, my shop has plenty of time to gear up for loading that cartridge. We are already making the casings in limited supply, and send some to Winchester, plus we are slowly building our inventory of casings."

"I see, how could I interest you in loading, say 25,000 rounds, so I can use them to entice shops to preorder this revolutionary pistol." "Sorry, not going to happen. I am not in the business of selling ammo to gun manufacturers—we only sell to gun shops in Texas and Colorado. We did sell a large order to Winston, but that's because we shoot with his town team and it is a personal matter. Yet Winston was told that any other orders would have to come from gun shops."

"Besides, where did you get those ammo boxes that Winston had to try them out with his entire team?" "I have an arrangement with a trade school in El Paso that manufactures 45ACP as part of their regular course. Then I use a gun shop next door to load them up for special advertising events. The yield is low, that's why I need 25,000 a month from you." "Interesting, now what do you do for cases once that class graduates?" "I'd have to wait six months or more for the next class. Now, I'm trying to convince this class to buy a 5-man brass fabricator and go into business to make me some 45ACP casings. All of this is tentative, and I'd rather deal directly with you."

"As I said, don't wait for us. I am very independent, and deal only with Winchester because of a mutual benefit. For now, you'd best be pushing your New Service 1898 DA push out cylinder in 38 or 44 special, because by next May their sales will crash. My shop is in full swing making 38 and 44 special casings and loading them for sale. We'll also anticipate this market to fall apart within a year, and we'll be ready by January to convert our loading section over to 45ACP. I also have to admit that I am entertaining six of the El Paso college boys that are willing to move to Dallas—so I doubt we are wooing the same bunch as you are. Anyway, good luck and we'll carefully watch your advertising progress."

"Oh, by the way, how is Ike Webb doing, and how did you steal him from me?" "He is doing very well, he went thru 100 gun shops in Denver, went thru 37 more in Colorado Springs/Pueblo/Trinidad, and he's now heading to New Mexico's 17 gun shops to include: Las Vegas, Raton, Santa Fe, and Albuquerque. Then he'll be working the Texas gun shops for a special purpose. I stole him from you, not because we offer the same salary, but we offer benefits that protect his nearly blind wife. Colt is behind the industry, and will eventually have to start providing benefits other than just wages." "Ok, well, I don't have control over the lack of benefits. Anyways, if you change your mind, you know how to reach me."

After Alden left, Amy came to see Sam. "We have a change in prices. The cost of bullets and powder has gone up almost 15%. Strangely enough, both Missouri Lead and Dupont Powder are offering us a two-year contract to avoid other price increases." "Sounds like the work of a certain Ira Winchester, heh?" "Yes, I'm sure you're right. So what do we do?" "We sign the contract and increase the price on our ammo boxes to $3 for 38s, and $3.50 for 44s. That will be in line for a year from now when we'll sell 45ACP ammo at $4 a box as we are currently taking preorders thru Ike."

Sam then went to help Ann at supervising the four new loading recruits. Amy was on the typewriter preparing an insert that notified buyers that their next order reflected a new price change caused by the increase in the price of components. Luke was already setting type as Amy was typing away. All orders, starting today, would have the enclosed notice with the new order forms. The next day, Irene started stuffing envelopes with these two publications, and addressing them to Texas gun shops.

*

It was Thursday afternoon, and the Duo was at the train depot to greet those six college boys from El Paso. After long introductions to get at least the students' first names, Sam took over the discussion. "Let's get you settled in your hotel rooms, then we'll meet in the hotel's bar to have a chat."

"Your three meals a day are included but here is $50 each for spending money. I remember when I was a college student, and two-bits in your pocket was a lot of money. So, it's ok to do some splurging. Now, let me go thru the salary and benefits we offer.............In return, the shop starts at 8AM, and closes at 5PM. You will all be placed on the brass fabrication of 45ACP cartridges as well as certified on the easier 38 and 44 special. This is the daily schedule we have planned for you: Tonight, get some rest and get acquainted with your room and restaurant. Tomorrow morning we test you on the 38 special fabricator. At noon we'll have a catered lunch and social hour to meet the other workers and some of the new women. The afternoon would include a tour of the shop."

"Saturday morning we'll give you a tour of the town, and then the city. The afternoon and evening are your private time, but many workers go dancing at the town hall which includes dance lessons and dinner. Sunday morning Amy and I will join you for breakfast at this restaurant. Then you have to choose—you're either returning June 1st or not. If you are returning, we will then discuss the moving and provide contracts. Then at noon you take the train back to El Paso to finish your training."

Amy added, "we are aware, that Alden Pickett is trying to convince you to buy a fabricator and go into business. Just remember, that it takes money to start a business. A safer route is to start with us to get experience and know-how. What we offer is a nice place to work and nice people to work with. We prefer you don't join us if you have doubts, because it is a big change from El Paso, as it may be a permanent change. Of interest, we are receiving 7 college men from Houston within two weeks on May 1st. So, you would have plenty of workers your age. So, good luck and we'll see you tomorrow morning."

That afternoon, most of the guys took a nap and had gathered in the restaurant at 7PM. They had just barely finished their steaks when six young women appeared at their table. One gal became the spokesman as she said, "the six of us have designated ourselves your official 'welcome party.' So, spread out and make room for us, and we'd enjoy coffee and dessert." As the restaurant turned out to be somewhat rowdy, the group was moved onto the bar for more socializing and laughing. Only days later did the group realize that sitting in the bar was now by couples—the restaurant visits had already led to some natural selection.

Arriving at their usual 7AM time, the Duo was surprised to see a bunch of their people already waiting to enter. By 8AM, the six college boys were let loose on the 38 special machine. The boys were surprised to have a 20-minute break at 10AM. By noon, Elton was giving a thumbs up to all six men. The social hour consisted of beer for the men and wine for the gals. The college boys could not believe that the first Friday of each month included a catered luncheon or an evening supper.

The tour started in A-wing where the 34 loaders were busy. The college boys were mesmerized by the process and could not believe that with the pull of the cycling arm, a new round fell into the bucket. Moving over to the processing tables, they were somewhat surprised to see the many cases being prepared. On way to B-Wing, they saw a full loading area. The boys were put thru the machine shop and finally found out what the men were machining. Neil brought them to the processing center and showed them the finished product—a progressive press. Soon, these presses would be put on the market. Of course, the next stop was Glen's machine making 45ACP casings. The last part of the tour including Kent loading a 300-pound crate of brass buds and heading for the warehouse. As the doors opened, there were several gasps and words of astonishments. Kent placed the crate on the third and top layer. Luke then gave the boys a tour of the different crates that were being stored for future use. This included the special section of 45ACP components. They were amazed on the well-built standing shelves full of components. At the end of the tour, the Duo knew that they had hooked a few good men.

The Saturday morning tour was done by 10AM and the boys wanted to visit the available boarding houses. The houses cost $40 a month but included two hot meals a day, a packed cold lunch for noon, power and heat. A laundry service was available for a one-time pickup at $1 a week. As pointed out, apartments were the same price but did not include lights, heat, food, and home cooking—a no brainer for single mem making $100 a month. The boys liked several of the boarding houses and somehow left a message to the owners that they would contact them come Sunday morning.

By 4PM, the Duo said, "Ok boys, you are on your own for tonight, and we'll see you in the morning. It's decision time, heh?" As the evening progressed, the Holts and Smiths joined them for their evening of dining and dancing. It was a surprise to see the six college boys enter with six of the single gals that were their own loaders. It was Ann who was first to speak, "well it looks like you just filled your fabricating staff to the max—better bring some contracts tomorrow morning."

After a fantastic evening of dancing, the Duo was glad to hit their bed for a welcome sleep. The next morning, they grabbed their briefcase and headed to the hotel's restaurant. "Good morning, I saw that you all learned how to do the waltz and the two step, heh?" "Yes, and it was a beautiful evening with nice people." "Ok, it's time to 'fish or cut bait' as they say. So, how say you individually."

One man said, "I speak for the six of us when I say that we are very impressed with your business and the community. It is clear in our minds that we desperately want to move to town and take the job offer, if you still want us." "Oh yeah, we need you and want you." "We only have one question, were you the ones who sent that welcoming party to our supper table last Thursday night—all six single gals from the shop?" The Duo looked at each other in total shock. Amy said, "we swear to God, we had nothing to do with that, and didn't know of the event till now." "Good, it paid off and we're glad they showed up, since we are slow with the social graces. Now this is another reason to move to Dallas, heh? As you say."

Sam was next to speak, I have an arrangement with three of the boarding houses, since they will have some of our workers arriving from Houston. I will reserve you all a spot when you arrive. Moving is expensive so here is $200 each to use as you see fit but most new worker buys an outfit upgrade, and a pistol for self-defense. You will be living close enough to work that you won't need a horse for now. So, sign your contract in duplicate, and keep the bottom copy for your records. See you in June."

The Duo went home to rest the remainder of the day. They were facing a meeting with Ike, and an over-load of orders to process. In two weeks, the seven graduates from Houston would be arriving, and who knew what else was in the cards.

***

CHAPTER 6

On Texas Ground

The next morning Esmerelda arrived early with a face free of bruises. She was greeted by Ann and all her coworkers. Although the reason for her disability had never been discussed, it was assumed that everyone knew—as everyone knew how their bosses had brought the cause to an end—at least for Esmerelda.

After the team got to work, Ike Webb showed up for his end of Colorado and New Mexico visit. "Welcome home Ike, this is your week off at home, as it is well earned." Amy took over, looking at the ledger she said, "you visited 100-gun shops in Denver, 37 shops between Colorado Springs and Trinidad, and 14 shops in Northern New Mexico. And you did it all in 20 workdays plus three weeks off." "That was a nice job starting the meeting before I could bring up the subject of an anonymous benefactor who paid off my mortgage and shocked the hair off my wife's upper lip—that was mighty nice, and I'm not about to forget it. Now, on to the meeting."

Sam continued, "we can't even tabulate the total for all the orders we're still getting and we're still 40 orders behind. Our records show an escrow account of +- $10,000 for 150 prepaid presses with kits. Unbelievably, we also have a separate escrow account of $49,000 for prepaid 45ACP ammo." "Yes, and they were all warned that we did not expect to start production until next year, but would at least be available before the pistols were released."

"Ok, so you did a great job. Now, we have two issues to discuss. What are your thoughts about when to release the BP presses." "I strongly feel you should start shipping them tomorrow." "Wow, that was with vigor, now why?" "It's simple, the people who buy your loaded smokeless ammo are not the same customers who use BP ammo. The everyday rancher, municipal day worker, teenager, and anyone who likes to plink will only afford to buy BP reloads at $1.50 a box when they earn $2.50 a day. The people who buy your more expensive ammo have the new VP certified pistols, have better things to do with their time than to clean guns, are not interested in reloading, and all earn $5 a day or more. Actually many are businessmen, ranch barons, professionals, oil barons, or those in speed shooting clubs. The other reason is that the gun shop owners need the extra income. Reloading ammo is a daily duty of all their trained employees, just like you and Neil did when you worked for George Whitehouse. Besides, you must have a heck of an inventory of presses ready to be shipped, heh?" "Yes, we have all the 150 units with the accessory kits already in boxes and addressed to the gun shop's destination." Sam got Amy's nod and added, "You have a strong argument, and you are likely right. We'll get all those ready units off this week."

"And I suspect the other issue is, what happens to me now? Do I hang up my sales-ability and join your loading team?" "No way, we need to keep you on the road." "Good, that's where I like to be." Sam then took over. "We'd like you to visit every large city in Texas. In reality Colorado and New Mexico have been exposed to smokeless ammo, the reloading presses and the upcoming 45ACP ammo. Now, Texas has only been exposed to our advertisements for smokeless ammo. It is time for them to see our own salesman and be exposed to our BP reloading press and to the upcoming ammo. We think you should start in Dallas where there are 42,000 people, and Fort Worth with its 24,000 people. That roughly breaks down to an estimated 45-gun shops in our back yard. Afterwards, you choose your city, but here is the population breakdown: San Antonio 53K, Houston 46K, El Paso 42K, Galveston 37K, Austin 22K, Laredo 14K, Brownsville 7K, and Corpus Christi 5K."

Ike was stunned as he said, "just the large cities basically boil down to 200-gun shops. How do you reach the other shops, we have 3 million people in Texas? The next category is 2,500 to 5,000 population, on the rail line, and we have at least 100 more-gun shops in this category. Plus we have a book prepared for you with all the owners, street addresses and even the phone numbers when possible. Keep in mind that some of these shops did not get our new price list for ammo—that is $3 for 38's, $3.50 for 44's, and the new $4.50 for prepaid 45ACP ammo."

"Amy wonders if the $4.50 is too high?" "Heck no, these people don't care what the price will be to keep that semi-automatic pistol shoot and shoot and shoot, heh? To me, what is more important is the new prices for 38's and 44's. The revolver enthusiasts, will be buying the new 1898 DA (double action) revolver in 38 special and with a push out cylinder, and this will keep the market going even with the new pistol."

"To summarize, we want you to become the Texas salesman for our products, and we want the Texas gun shops to know that you are the sole representative on the road for this company. We figure a full paid day every two weeks for answering any communications that arrive by either postal mail or telegram. We don't think you should mention this service during your visits. As a precaution against emergencies, we will at least read your telegrams and mail, but leave the responses to you. So this current assignment consists of +-300-gun shops, but set over a lot of territory along the rail line. At 4 gun shops a day, you could be done in 15 weeks, but because of the extensive traveling, it could be 4 weeks longer."

"Sounds great, I'll start in town next Monday. I presume, we'll continue our meetings the Monday of my 3 days' off?" "Yes, and good luck/stay safe." Amy added, "the number of days off is up to you, heh?"

*

Irene was glad to be shipping the presses, since she was running out of room in the B-Wing storage room. She was able to place 8 units in each crate as long as they were all going to the same city. Within the week, all 150 prepaid presses were shipped out. The 34 loaders were putting out 68,000 rounds a day and the processing team was boxing them into 1,360 fifty round boxes each day. With the fixed rate boxes full, Amy was addressing the FR-50 boxes, adding a new price list and order form—the Texas addresses also had a note that a company representative would be visiting them soon. Luke was always nearby to take the addressed 50-pound boxes to the loading area, and keep her table free to work.

Sam was watching the system in progress. With a surplus of 38 and 44 casings, the loaders were kept at bay by the aggressive processing tables now well manned by Ida, Lucille, Hans, Edna, and occasionally Irene or Luke. It was Sam who told Amy that night, "every section is on 'ground.' They are functioning efficiently and at their maximum. The fabricators and machinists will have to be temporarily reorganized once the Houston college boys arrive, and again in June with the arrival of six more brass fabricators."

At the end of the week was payday on Thursday, and the foremen's meeting Friday morning. As usual, once the teams were started, the foremen gathered in the office around the meeting table. Sam started the meeting. "As you all know we now have bars on the windows and a security system with night watchmen from 5PM to 7AM. The guards are complaining that too many employees are returning to the shop because they forget something at their station. The guards have no way of knowing whether these people actually work here, so they follow them and document what they take and where they got it, as well as get some name—whether it is true or fictitious."

"So to get this under control we will be issuing a pocket Id card with name, employee number and a current photograph. Without this card, no one will be allowed to enter from now on. Also, please tell the workers in your section to minimize coming back, one of these days someone will get shot as an intruder—these watchmen are armed, and we have them because of the large inventories of expensive components."

Before I start with each of you, I've decided to add a suggestion box next to the lunchroom, and offer $25 to anyone who provides a suggestion that we implement. So, please inform your workers. Now let's begin with:"

Neil—"We have 7 new Houston college boys arriving next weekend. Four in brass fabrication and three in machining. As I will explain shortly, for the next week and today, move Elmer, Paul, Vern, and Finley into brass fabrication. That will leave you and Titus in machining and you should use your time to make the most difficult press part until the college boys arrive so you can start them on easier parts. When the boys arrive, bring back Vern and Finley and add Titus to supervise the three boys. When these boys can work independently, please move Vern and Finley back to brass fabrication."

"Now let me explain to you and everyone here why the push to move men back to the brass machines. We now have five machines in operation and need these four machinists to man machine #5. Machine #6 will be ready by Thursday just before the Houston boys arrive. Now with all six machines in operation, we can generate 30,000 casings a day. The problem is that with, 34 loaders putting out 2,000 rounds each day, that comes to 68,000 rounds a day. I'd say that is about 2:1 ratio, and if it wasn't for the 1 million cases in storage, we wouldn't be able to put out the orders from

Colorado or New Mexico. This surplus is already down to a half million, and we need to minimize its discrepancy as much as possible. I may also add that Ike starts in Texas on Monday and will be our salesman throughout the state—he will concentrate in selling the press and prepaid orders for the 45ACP, now at $4.50 a box. I'm certain that he'll also generate more orders on the 38 and 44s—so expect plenty of BP press orders. And Irene, go ahead and ship them out as soon as Neil says they are ready." "Great plan Sam, I may shed a tear when I lose those experienced machinists, but Titus and I will manage with the new machinists."

Glen—"Now you see the need for casings. So use the 75,000 surplus 45ACP casings to send 25,000 a month to Winchester. That will free you up for the next three months to make 38 and 44 casings." "Out of the need to plan, how many rounds does that $49,000 escrow account from Colorado/New Mexico come to in rounds?" "At the $4 rate they were charged, it comes to 612,500 rounds, or +-10 days of loading—considering there are always down days with illness, personal days, and pregnancy/maternity days."

Ann—"I have all 34 loaders working with no pregnancy on the horizon." Laughter covers the entire table. "But we have to expect that this will be happening soon, and it will start with morning sickness, and then fatigue, back ache, urinary frequency and so on, but we'll do our best to manage.

Getting back on track, I have chosen Craig Dufield as my assistant supervisor. He is supervising as we meet today. He is very knowledgeable, pleasant, and trustworthy." Amy interjected, "that is great, just let me know when he supervises so I can adjust his pay, and it doesn't matter if it's an hour or a full day."

Irene—"You're next. Let's start with a new category. Please tell us what our inventory is up to." "Well there are two categories, a daily replacement inventory and a surplus category. The replacement category is a half million pieces of primers, bullets, and brass buds, plus the half million equivalent of powder and brass fabrication materials, and of course the half million 38 and 44 casings. Now, the surplus is a million units of primers, bullets, brass buds, and the equivalent in powder and processing materials. PLUS, we have the new category of 45ACP components, with is already up to a half million for each component—but missing the casings, heh?"

"Next, I have shipped all presses/kits to Colorado and New Mexico. I am still keeping an inventory of 100 press frames, and generally reorder when down to 50 frames—the turn-around is less than a week from the Houston Foundry."

"I have received those two dozen four die sets of 45ACP loading dies from L. Lofton with a note that said 'very smart move, and Uncle Ira is very pleased with those 25,000 casings he gets from you each month.'"

"Next, I am hearing rumors that our brass bud supplier, Union Metal out of Oregon, is talking 'strike' from workers demanding benefits. Any direction what we should do or not do?" Amy answered, "send a telegram today to Ira Winchester, and ask him if he heard the rumors. If true, can he suggest a second supplier, so we don't have all our eggs in one basket."

"Good idea, well I have many orders out so we'll keep adding to that fantastic warehouse. My last issue is a point of contention. After the last time you two and Glen took off to capture those bank robbers, I promised myself that the next time I would be there to cover Glen and your backs. That is not negotiable, so don't try to change my mind. If something ever happened to you three and I wasn't there to help—well forget it. So, in case that ever happened, we need to name someone who would become the automatic business manager in charge. Any ideas who that should be?" Silence fell upon the room as Neil finally said, "I think it should be a family member, either one of the Barkers or Elmer." Luke and Ida looked at each other and both nodded. Luke said, "it would be an honor, but we feel it should be Elmer who has more experience than we do."

Sam whispered to Amy and announced that Elmer would be the acting manager if the four of them were out of the shop at the same time. Luke added, "and I feel that he should now be at all our foremen's meetings." "I agree, let's take a break. I'll go talk with him and if he accepts the responsibility, we'll bring him up to date on this meeting and have him join us for the remainder of the meeting."

The meeting resumed with a new member. Sam then went with:

Luke and Ida—"you're next. Ida said, "we are good. With Lucille, Hans, and the new Edna, as well as the occasional Irene and Luke, we can actually process those 68,000 rounds a day—which comes to 1,360 ammo boxes a day. By the way, we are now up to six high school, boys and now girls, to put together those +-1,400 boxes every day after school. Also, those 1,360 ammo boxes translate to 57 fixed rate boxes, along with Irene's packed presses/kits, that we ship every day with a morning pickup. After lunch, the freight delivery rail car arrives for unloading which keeps Kent busy till 3 or 4PM."

Luke had a subject to discuss. "We've been offered to retrofit our three expediting wagons and our new hydraulic lift with an electric motor powered by a rechargeable 12-volt battery. For sure, Kent needs it on his hydraulic lift that hauls 300 pounds all over the shop to get to the warehouse, and Irene and I would also appreciate it. The cost is $150 per wagon—installed." Sam added, "of course, go ahead and do it. I may add that the warehouse looks good the way you stack crates three high, keep moving forward towards the aisle, and only have rows of the same items. It makes locating and maintaining an inventory easy that way. Tell Kent, good job."

"Well Elton, last but not least. What have you got for us?" "I am in total awe the way you run this meeting and clearly direct the business on its proper path. It is obvious that all eyes will be on this fabrication department in the short and long term. So, with the college boys arriving this weekend and the next bunch in one month, it is time for me to step down, and it's the perfect time to put a young man in charge. So, I ask that you put Glen in charge, and I'd be happy to continue working in this department." There was total silence as people started to voice their opinions. *He's right, agree, time is perfect, good point Elton, the younger foreman can best relate with young workers, and Glen is more than capable.*

Sam finally spoke, "well Glen are you ready and willing?" "Yes, and I'd be happy to take over." Elton added, "before I leave the foremanship, I have a couple of recommendations. With cousins that work in the Houston College and in Big Blue's factory in Arizona, I have two recommendations. The first, apparently two of the machinists have been spending a lot of time in the brass fab lab and might be willing to change from machining to brass fab. The other is planning for the future.

My cousin said that the small factory is putting out a new 5-man machine every week. They have 20 machines completed and are still going at $5,000 each. It is predicted that when the 45ACP cartridge is out, that the price will go up to $7,000 per machine, and with a long back order list. So my recommendation is as follows:

1. There is plenty of room to duplicate the front row, on the back wall, with as much as six additional machines. If you have the money, order two more in 45ACP—now while the price is good and supply is available.

2. Having two extra machines unmanned is a waste. So notify the El Paso and Houston colleges that you need 10 men trained in brass fabrication by next Xmas when they have their half year graduations. To help this along, you can offer to fund some students in financial need to guarantee training in brass fab—etcetera if you get my drift?

3. If you do get 10 workers next Xmas, I think your 38 and 44 orders will start dwindling down and you'll be starting to make 45ACP since it will take six months to build your own inventory before you start loading the new round."

"And so, this department will grow under Glen's direction. I also agree that it is time to pull all capable brass fabricators out of the machining section till you have control of supply over demand."

After a silent period, Sam addressed Amy, "well dear, it is your turn and time to close this meeting. "Ok, just to let everyone know that Rosie's Cleaning Service starts next week. Tuesday and Thursday evenings for a light pickup and cleaning, with the big cleanup on Saturday. Also, things are changing with Cyrus. He is acting as our messenger, driver, and shotgun guard for Irene or me. He doesn't have time to take care of every horse and buggy, so ask your workers to pool their rides. All men will now have to take care of their horses, and Cyrus will help as many ladies as he can—and any lady who can care for their horses should do so. Also, we are offering time and a half to any fab worker that is willing to work for the extra cash this and every Saturday—and Sam will be one of the fabricators." Sam whispered to Amy as she came back, "we are in so much need for casings, that anyone working a full day on Saturday will earn $10, double time, as well as all future Saturdays till we catch up."

Sam closed with, "good meeting, let's go to work."

*

The next morning, Sam went to work. When he arrived, every fab worker was present, and all five machines had a full team of 5 men. Amy and Irene had stayed home to do some housework, cooking, and laundry. By 1PM the Twins, as Amy and Irene were getting to be called, were scheduled to meet the college boys from Houston, and get them placed in their assigned boarding houses, and provide what guidance they needed.

The Twins went to Darcy's for lunch and were by the train platform before the train arrived. As they walked on the platform, they couldn't believe their eyes. Seven of the new loaders were already there waiting for the train. Irene finally asked, "what is this, why are you here?" "We're waiting for our men, it's been several weeks of postal communications, and it's time to be together."

As the men disembarked, the gals were clearly more than friends. Finally Amy took over, "excuse me, but we need to pair up. We have three boarding houses, two with double occupancy and one with a triple. After the assignments were done, two men came over and asked, "we went back to school and changed our majors from machining to fabrication and wondered if we could do a lateral change before starting work?"

After getting the nod from Amy, Irene said, "yes, I will inform my husband tonight and you can start in fabrication on Monday—by the way my husband is Glen, and he is your new foreman effective today." Amy added, "now, you are on your own till Monday, and I see you won't be alone with all the ladies to keep you company. Enjoy your weekend."

Come 5PM, Sam and Glen came crawling home after a long profitable day at work. With their hot bath waiting, the Duos were off by 6PM to the townhall for dinner and dancing.

Sunday was another needed day at home to recover. Breakfast became brunch and by noon, the Duo got dressed. It was Sunday dinner at the Barkers and the Duo was not about to miss this gathering—now including Elmer and Lucille as a couple. It wasn't long into the dinner that Amy finally blurted it out, "ok you two, time to get clean, when are you announcing your engagement and when is the wedding?" Lucille said, "what is the rush, we have all summer." "No you don't. Look around at work, and I bet that half those new faces will wed this summer. If you want a diner to host your reception, you need to schedule it and even schedule the minister as well. So, before we leave here today, I will have a date in my scheduling pad, heh?" "For sure, daughter-in-law!"

The week was going well. Titus was training Stu, the new worker, as all the other original essential workers were supervising the other six fab workers. Things were going smooth till Wednesday AM, when Amy realized that she had forgotten the office ledger at home. So, after finding, Cyrus, they went back to the house to get the ledger.

Forty-five minutes later, Amy wasn't back, so Ida came to find Sam supervising the new fab workers. "Sam, something is wrong. Amy and Cyrus left 45 minutes ago to pick up the ledger from your house, and they are not back, I'm worried." Sam took off like lightening, took the nearest saddled horse, and took off at a full gallop with his pistol at his side. Arriving at the house, Cyrus was lying on the driver's seat and unconscious. Sam ran to the house, but the door was locked. Getting inside, the ledger was still on the kitchen table and Sam knew what had happened.

When Sam got back outside, Sheriff Wilson and his deputy, who had been summoned by a worried neighbor, had just arrived to awaken Cyrus. "Cyrus, what happened?" "No idea, Amy had just hopped off the buggy when everything went black, and here you and the sheriff are looking over me."

"Amy has been kidnapped, Charlie would you go to Sil's ranch and get him and Two Cloud. And Sheriff, I'll need your brother, Wil. We'll all gather at the house in one hour. The sheriff escorted Cyrus back to the shop as Sam came running in the shop where the Barkers, Holts, and Elmer with Lucille were anxiously waiting. Sam was to the point, "Amy has been kidnapped and I'm going after them. These kidnappers are going to die one way or another, I prefer they die on the gallows, but that may not be possible, especially if the leader is who I think he is." "Are you waiting for a ransom request?" "Heck no, we're going to push hard and be at their camp or hideout by dark." "Glen and Irene, will you join me?"

"Of course, we just need to pick up our gear, horses, pistols and pump shotguns." "Then Elmer, everything is on your shoulders, whatever you decide is final. Your name was added on the business account at the Wells Fargo, and if there is something you don't know, just ask any of our foremen." "Got it, and be safe, but bring back my daughter-in-law, heh?" "I will or die trying."

*

Sam had Guard saddled and loaded with emergency gear and two long guns—his pump shotgun and his scoped 30-30. Glen and Irene were also ready when Wil showed up ready to ride. Arriving at a full gallop was the deputy with Keith Turner, Sil's foreman, and Two Cloud. Keith spoke first, "Sil is in Kansas selling off some stock, so I am representing him, and I am not going back." Meanwhile Two Cloud was looking at the tracks. "Five horses plus one horse and buckboard. Horses' hoofs are overgrown over worn shoes. We can follow them but will have to check ground often to not get off the trail—I can do it for Missy! We can ride hard, while we start watching the buckboard tracks in the road, till they dump it and go cross country."

Before the group took off, Two Cloud requested a piece of Miss Amy's used clothing before washing off the body scent. Sam went inside and took a riding skirt out. Giving it to Two Cloud, he smelled every part of the skirt. Afterwards, Sam took off after Two Cloud, as the posse consisting of Wil, Keith, Glen and Irene, followed at a full gallop. It was two hours before they spotted an area where the outlaws and the buckboard had veered off the road. The buckboard was found hidden in the trees as an extra horse for the buckboard driver was brought out of hiding, and the harness horse was likely saddled for Amy. As the six horses headed cross country, Two Cloud suddenly stopped and picked up a 2+ inch piece of fine white cotton. Two Cloud smelled it and said, "it's Miss Amy."

The posse looked at each other and Sam finally said, "that's a smart woman, unless I'm mistaken, that is part of her under panties. She is leaving us trail markers"—Two Cloud nodded in agreement.

Meanwhile earlier, Amy who had been knocked out and blind-folded, was now alert as the kidnappers stopped to change to riding horses instead of the buckboard. Her hands were now tied in front of her as the blindfold was removed. "So, it's you again, Bull. Well, this time Sam will kill you." "Shut up you bitch, and get on the horse." "Not before I go pee." As Amy was brought to the bushes, she did her business as she tore off her panties and stuffed pieces in her bra. As she was getting on her horse, her hands rubbed against her right front pocket revealing the pleasant surprise—her derringer was still in the pocket of her riding skirt.

The posse proceeded slower for fear of riding right into an ambush. For hours, the posse kept seeing those white pieces of cloth on the ground. It was clear that Amy was being trailed on a rope as the last rider, to be able to drop those striking markers, without being detected. Things were going well when they came to a brook and stopped to water their horses. Two Cloud kept sniffing the air when he finally said, "I can smell chimney soot, we could be close to this outlaw camp." Sam thought a bit, and finally said, "assuming these are our kidnappers, they will be sending a man to leave a ransom demand, since this is the first chance they've had to do so. We need to intercept this messenger before he sees us and warns his cohorts with a gunshot. Besides knowing what to expect at the cabin makes it safer for us as we arrive to free Amy."

After hiding the horses, everyone stretched out on the trail ready to capture the kidnapper at gun point. Two Cloud chose a large hardwood tree overlooking the trail and was hidden high amongst the branches. Hours went by when a single rider was seen approaching. Two Cloud was the first to greet him. As the rider appeared under the tree, Two Cloud dropped onto the rider's saddle—coming face to face with the outlaw. All the facial paint made Two Cloud look like the "death warrior." Sam later recalled the sequence of events. "As the Indian's face appeared inches away from the unsuspecting miscreant, the outlaw's face distorted out of reality, the man moved his bowels, and Two Cloud popped his war club on the white man's nose—just enough to knock him out."

When the outlaw woke up, Sam was holding the ransom note asking $50,000. "I see you are awake, so listen to me carefully, I want to know how many outlaws are holding my wife, is my wife ok, and what was Bull going to do with her. If you don't answer my questions, we're going to let the Indian at you, he'll start by scalping you and do things that no human should ever endure." "Without warning, Two Cloud jumped on his chest and cut an ear off. The gagged outlaw tried to yell but only managed a groan thru his gag. After he stopped moaning, Sam asked him if he was ready to talk. The outlaw nodded yes.

"There are four other men who are all wanted men in Oklahoma. They are all gunfighters that won't go down easy. The leader you already know as Efrain Bull. We were planning to split the ransom, and then sell your woman to a 300-pound monster, hung like a horse, who goes thru women by tearing them up as he rapes them. She was worth another $5,000 to that animal. Now keep that Indian away."

The outlaw was tied up, gagged, his ear stump cauterized, and left in camp. With the horses tethered in good grass with fresh water, the posse headed for the outlaw's cabin. It was a half hour walk when the cabin was spotted. As darkness was falling, the posse was hidden behind the privy. It was several hours when Amy pushed one of the outlaws to let her go to the privy. "Hurry up." Amy entered the privy as the escorting outlaw had a sudden appearance of a face out of hell, as he then collapsed to the ground with a forehead bashed into his brain.

When Amy opened the privy door, she was greeted by an angel, as Irene grabbed her and brought her to safety in Sam's arms. After kissing and plenty of tears, Amy said, "did you bring my pistol." Sam thought it was an odd request, so he said, "sure, I'll trade you for your panties." "Heck, you already got them in pieces, heh?"

The kidnappers were still asleep when Two Cloud arrived with a sac alive with some animal. "What have you got there?" "A very upset 'badger." We throw in cabin and let it do its thing—fight, bite, and claw at the bunch. As the outlaws come out, we arrest or shoot them." "How do you know he will attack them?" "Watch—as he starts to kick the animal thru the sac. I kick him in the 'balls,' sore 'nuts' really get him mad, heh?"

The posse got lined up for a gunfight as Two Cloud threw the sac into the cabin and ran away. A few minutes later he heard a screech and an animal howl as the outlaws started screaming. The badger was biting and chewing off body parts. Someone yelled "shoot that thing—BANG. You fool you just shot me in the foot." The attack continued as someone yelled, "let's get out of here."

When the outlaws saw there was a posse waiting, they all made a quick decision and decided to fight their way to freedom. The posse responded with pump shotguns as all three kidnappers and Bull went down. The only living one was Bull who had taken Buckshot to a shoulder, and the ball had been pulverized to bone chips. Bull kept screaming out in pain when Two Cloud asked, "is this the woman beater I heard about?" "Amy answered, "yes, the beast that he is!"

After checking the dead outlaw's pockets, and removing their gunbelt/pistols, they were loaded and secured onto their horses. Finding some rifles in the cabin, they were added to the pack horse's paniers. It was Glen who finally asked, referring to Bull, "what do we do with this piece of trash?"

Two Cloud had decided that justice had to be done. Without warning, he jumped on Bull, grabbed a handful of hair, passed his knife in several directions, and pulled the scalp up with a loud pop. Bull's scream made the tree leaves quiver and Keith lost his breakfast.

After the sight of a bone-bald Bull had settled, Glen said, "why don't you all start walking back to our horses, and let me take care of this turd." Amy responded, "I appreciate your offer, but it is up to Sam and me to finish this. So go ahead and we'll catch up later." With the posse and the dead outlaws gone, the Duo was facing a decision.

Sam said, "do we have the right to kill him, or should we load him up and bring him to hang?" "I told him weeks ago that if he returned to Dallas, that I would kill him. He was planning for me to have the death of a martyr, he's evil, and needs to meet his maker with the look of 'fear on his face.' So, this is my answer." Amy tied his hands behind his back and then pulls her derringer, steps up to Bull, and shoots both his kneecaps off. Bull went berserk, now with a bleeding scalp line, a blown-out shoulder, and both knees bleeding, Amy said, "we can leave now."

The posse was still in earshot, as they heard the two gunshots. As the Duo started walking away, everyone heard, "hey, you can't leave me here without a gun, I can't walk, and the wolves will come. Stop, come back. Come back............"

The Duo had taken a dozen paces when Amy stopped and said, "I can't do it. Being eaten alive is cruel and excessive torture on humans. It is actually on the same level as the execution torture during Medieval times when four horses were tied to the condemned hands and feet and quartered till the extremities were pulled off the body, or the same as savages burning a white man's legs off till the meat fell off the bone. We are better than that."

Amy took the outlaw pistol out of the back of Sam's gunbelt. She then ejected all the shells and reinserted one live round in the cylinder and rotated the cylinder so the next shot would be the live round. The Duo then went back to Bull, cut the piggin strings, and freed his hands. Amy made it clear to Bull, "there is one live round in this revolver. Use it wisely when the wolves arrive. This is intended to be a mercy move on my part. Before you pull the trigger, remember that I forgive you as you have the chance to ask for God's forgiveness. If you use it to shoot Sam or me, as we leave, then you will be eaten alive—and that is a promise."

After the Duo caught up with the posse, everyone heard the howl of a pack of wolves as the sound of devouring animals fell upon the true beast. As there was an increase in animal sounds, there came a hideous scream followed by one clear—BANG. It was Irene that said, "Amy, you are a good person, that was a mercy shot."

***

CHAPTER 7

Mid-Year and Beyond

The next morning the Duo came to work as usual. The workers greeted the bosses the usual way. After the starting bell was sounded, something unusual happened, every worker in the shop walked directly to Amy's processing table where the Duo was standing, and started with a soft applause that grew in intensity until Amy acknowledged them. Amy and Sam each said a few words and acknowledged the help from Wil, Two Cloud, Keith Turner, Glen, and Irene.

It was that afternoon when Sheriff Wilson arrived with the news. "Those five kidnappers were from Oklahoma, and were wanted men dead or alive, for marauding settlers and ranchers on the Kansas plains. They had left Kansas months ago when the law was getting too close, and were hiding in the Indian Nations. That is where Bull hired them. The bounty reward comes to $5,000 but coming from Kansas, it will take weeks to get the telegraph voucher. I've sold the guns and horses for a total of $700, so how do you want me to divide the $5,800?" "300 for you, $1,100 for Wil, Two Cloud, Glen, Irene, and Keith Turner." "Will do!"

The day was hectic as the orders were pouring in. Ike was getting an appreciative response. Every gun shop was prepaying for their press and kits, plus recognizing the value of prepaid orders for 45ACP—being the first customers to get their new ammo, and likely before the new pistols would even be on their shelves.

The one surprise this week was the two letters back from W. Winthrop c/o Houston college, and another letter from an Elroy Caruthers, headmaster of the El Paso College of Trades. The answer was the same, "we'd be happy to alert our entering students of your offer, its wages, and benefits—including the move to Dallas. Regarding your scholarship offer, can you be more specific? RSVP. Always W.W. and E.C."

Sam never hesitated, along with Amy's suggestion, wrote the same letter to both headmasters. "In regard to your question on my scholarship offer, it is quite simple. I will pay the tuition, books, room and board, to any student who is willing to move to Dallas and work in my Texas Load shop for the next eighteen months at full pay with all the benefits, a moving bonus of $200, and eligible for the six months bonuses that are part of profit sharing. If a student wants to join the program, I will pay their train fare and house them to come and see my shop and talk with the workers before they sign the contract and I shell out my part in fees."

Amy liked the letter and added, "this sounds so good, what happens if we get more than ten applicants." "We add another machine if that is the case. We'll manage." After this response, Sam instructed Irene to go ahead and order machine #7 and 8 in 45ACP.

A week later, a letter came from Ira Winchester. The Duo read:

> *Hello again,*
>
> *You are correct, Union Metal of Oregon is on the verge of a shutdown strike by the workers who want basic benefits. It is definitely time to order eggs from a different basket.*

We have other accounts that supply us brass buds, but I will only mention the ones west of the Mississippi. I refer to South Dakota Brass Incorporated. I've already mentioned that you are one of our partners and could be eligible for our present buying rate.

Simply order 500,000 at a penny a bud, include your $5,000 telegraph voucher, and that will establish your credit for the future. Then cut down your Union Metal orders accordingly, but keep both businesses on the books.

This idea of not putting all your eggs in the same basket is a wise idea. In that regard, I feel you need to have a second supplier of powder and hardcast lead bullets west of the Mississippi. My staff will be working on that, and I will be getting back to you on this matter.

In closing, the monthly 25,000 casings of 45ACP are of such excellent quality, that my quality assurance engineer simply opens your crate, laughs-out-loud, and has the crate stacked for future use.

As usual, thanks, and good luck.
Asa Winchester.

Again, Irene was given the letter and asked to put in the order. Irene then mentioned that California Powder Works had sent her several letters and amazing first order discounts. After discussing it, Irene was encouraged to go ahead and place an order for both the fast and medium powders to see if there was a savings compared with Dupont Powder. On the same note, Iowa had a new lead mine with high deposits of tin and antimony. Their bullet manufacturing plant was offering great discounts, so an order was prepared for all three bullet types: 125 gr. RN 38 sp. sized .358, 200 gr. RN 44 sp. sized .430, and 230 gr. RN 45ACP. sized .451 inch.

The weeks just rolled on. The Houston boys were doing well, and everyone was in a good mood. Before they knew it, the weekend had arrived when the six El Paso workers were arriving on the Saturday 1PM train. This time it was the Duo who was planning on welcoming them on the platform as they disembarked. Again, Amy commented on the female welcoming party. Sam thought a bit then said, "unless, I'm mistaken, we'll be attending several weddings this summer, heh?" "For sure!"

The month rolled by and it was time for the mid-year business meeting. The payday had just been held, and people were heading home. The next day, it would be work as usual from 8AM to 1PM, and then the social hour and complete dinner followed by the business meeting. Suddenly, the exodus stopped, and a bunch of young workers were huddled together near the processing tables. The Duo was then confronted by Neil and Ann as well as Glen and Irene. Glen was elected spokesman.

"Sam and Amy, we have been accosted by our workers, to discuss with them how to practice safe sex. We're aware that during vacation next week, that many of these couples will be moving together, etcetera. For the good of the company and peace of mind for our workers, we feel you two need to give the same lecture that you gave us some time ago. We all feel strong about this, that I am willing to pair up with Neil, as Irene will pair up with Ann, and we will present the facts as we are practicing. Yet, this very sensitive subject, we think, is best presented by you two—the shop owners who have more credibility than foremen. What say you?"

The Duo was pensive and looked over the group of young workers that they had chosen and hired at a young age. Amy gave the nod, and Sam said, "the men in the lunchroom with me, and the ladies in the office with Amy and with their own chairs from the lunchroom."

With everyone seated, Neil and Glen were listening at the door as they heard Sam say, "this is a very serious and sensitive subject, and I can only tell you what Amy and I have done at our doctor's suggestion, and it has now worked for almost two years. Jokes, comments, and laughter will not be allowed. Pull that crap and you're out of here. So, shut up and listen. After I'm done, we'll have a Q and A period when you'll be able to ask anything, since we don't want you to leave here with questions left on your mind. So, here goes." At that point the eaves-dropping foremen and forewomen closed the doors, and went to wait outside for the end of the meeting.

After the meeting, the crowd was still very solemn as they walked out in pairs. Irene asked how it went and Sam said, my group did well till I mentioned that brimming was dangerous to get an 'oops." For some reason that word tickles the men's fancy. Amy added, "strange, but that word scared my gals. What pushed them over the edge was when asked what to do with a woman that was slow to peak—when I said more assiduous foreplay by your man to get the woman begging for relief, the place cracked up. Anyways, it's done, so let's go home. Sam and I still have to prepare an agenda for tomorrow."

*

That night after dinner, the Duo prepared two agendas. The first was bonuses and the second was the general new information agenda. The Duo worked on the bonuses first. After agreeing on giving +-$20,000 in bonuses, they divided it as follows:

Early arrivals within 2 months 13X$100 = $1,300

Six-month workers 15X$200 = $3,000

One-year workers 35X$300 = $10,500

Essential workers or floaters 6X$400 = $2,400

Foremen and salesman 6X$500 = $3,000

TOTAL = $20,200 for 75 workers.

Afterwards, they set up an agenda of the many subjects to cover.

The day started on time, the 10 AM break was cancelled, and work continued right up to the noon bell. By then the beer and wine was flowing along with cheese and crackers. Everyone was in a good mood and plenty of socializing was about. It was the Duo who took a few minutes to contemplate what they saw. Sam said, "we have good people working for us, and this is a nice second family." Amy added, "this makes it a pleasure to come to work."

The social hour lasted till 2PM, and as the beer ran out the hot food arrived—baked ham, mashed potatoes, sweet raisin sauce, carrots, green bean creamy casserole, and homemade bread with butter. Plenty of coffee and tea, and a dessert surprise to follow. There was plenty of food, and seconds were common. Despite seconds, food was left over. The leftovers were boxed and were offered to workers with large families. Over a surprise dessert of apple pie with vanilla ice cream, and plenty of coffee/tea, Sam was ready to call the business meeting to order.

Amy and I are very happy to say that we are again profitable, and bonuses will be offered mid-year." Applause followed. "We will now start with the business agenda and save the bonuses for last. To everyone's surprise Elmer got up and said, "Lucille and I would like to announce that on Wednesday, during our vacation, we are getting married and everyone is invited." With a surprising applause, Cyrus got up, lifted his hand to quiet the crowd and said, "Esmerelda and I are also getting married on Wednesday—as a double ring ceremony." More vigorous applause. Cyrus added, "the marriage ceremony is at 9:30AM at St. Roger's church, and the reception is at the townhall. We'll have a social hour, and at noon, the townhall cooks will put on a chicken and dumplings dinner. We've hired the regular band and will have a dance party all afternoon." More applause. Elmer took over, "with your wives, significant others, and dates, we should be 125 people. Please, no gifts. Just join us for the celebration. Oh and by the way, older adults can also fall in love, heh?" More applause and whistles.

After the crowd simmered down, the Duo was seen whispering to each other, when Sam spoke up. "Amy and I fully realize that several weddings will likely be held this summer. With every worker's three personal days, a mid-week wedding could 'repeatedly' cripple the day's production at the shop. So, this is what we propose. Any worker who marries on a Saturday, we will give the couple three nights and two days in one of the better hotels in Dallas—it will include all meals, alcohol, and resident entertainment. Plus full pay till their return to work on Friday." This time the lunchroom was shaking with table pounding, whistles, guffaws, and loud applause.

Finally, order was restored, and Sam started the meeting. Amy went first:

1. "In the event of a sudden death of a worker, we have already promised that the dependents will receive 35% of the wage earner's pay till they become independent. But that does not cover paying off mortgages, debts, line of credits, clothing needs, house repairs, kids' education and so on. So, we are, effective today, adding a life insurance policy of $1,500 to all our workers." Applause started, but Ike and his wife were seen crying with joy. Sam took the next subject.

2. "Body odor (BO). The reality is that with 75 workers in the shop, we have a problem with air quality, especially with the summer at our doorsteps. If you do your part, we'll do ours. So, we ask of you to bathe every Sunday night, sponge bathe during week, wear deodorant called MUM which is available at

Asa's store. If you do this, during the vacation week, workers will be installing, in A-Wing, ceiling fans and air exhaust fans, like we have in B-Wing." More applause in approval.

3. Amy added, "also to help clean the air and control BO, we are adding a free uniform top with the company logo. These tops will be button up-front with one pocket and short sleeves—of course. They will be a soft cotton weave; you should change a least twice a week or as often as you want. We will store them in both restrooms in four universal sizes s, m, l, and xl—fits either men or women. Soiled ones go in the laundry basket and pickup and delivery will be daily. Please don't wear these company tops at home during nights and weekends. When in town on business or errands, please wear them to advertise our company. We are proud of you wearing them in public and hope you will be as well. In the winter, if you are cold, please add warmer underclothes, but always wear short sleeves when working."

4. "Cleaning service. Rosie's service is now coming Tuesdays and Thursdays to do their maintenance floor sweeping, clean toilets,

pick up garbage pails, and sweep all working benches and tables of debris. Then on Saturday, they do the major cleaning. They do all the Thursday activities as well as wash; all loading bench tops, worktables in B-Wing, the press processing table, and the general processing tables. They also replace any burnt out bulbs." Sam then took over.

5. "Your benefits status will change year to year. First of all, they will not be in perpetuity. They need to be approved each year by me and Amy, and yearly renewal depends on the business's continued profitability. For example, in extremes, if the business closes, don't expect your benefits to continue. As long as the yearly bottom line is in the black, your benefits will remain in full force—and we plan on being here a long, long time."

6. "Long term planning. Once I hear from Houston and El Paso regarding the potential for future workers, we will be adding fabricating machines on the back row to match the future number of oncoming workers—all for 45ACP. There is no doubt that we will eventually operate as a fabricating and loading company for the new caliber. When

that will happen, we'll keep you posted. As for the immediate months, we'll still be concentrating on fabricating and loading 38s and 44s."

"We are still selling presses to Texas gun shops, and once smokeless powder is available to gun shops, we'll start selling balance beam scales, priming systems, and powder measures to convert the BP presses to smokeless presses. With all the VP certified guns on the market, the black powder era will start to fade away. We have been told that all the new semi-automatic pistols will all be VP certified."

"So, before we move to bonuses, are there any questions?" Paul asked, "how committed are you to finding trained brass fabricators?" "100%, if Houston or El Paso bomb out, I will start advertising in all Arizona and California locations that have brass cartridge fabrication. I will then extend to other schools or factories west of the Mississippi. If I can't find any, we're going to hire machinists anywhere we can find them and train them in brass fabrication. Bottom line, We want to fill the back line with six machines, and find operators to man them. ASAP."

Elmer added, "so we are putting all our eggs in this 45ACP basket." "Yes and No. We will always sell 38s and 44s when the orders come in and with these new durable DA pistols (Colt's New Service and S&W triple lock) I am sure that orders will continue for decades. But these orders will not maintain a staff of 75 workers. Only a new demand for this semi-automatic pistol and its cartridge will keep us in full operation. In short, we'll be loading 45ACP and fabricating 45ACP cases for us and for sale to Winchester." After a long pause, with no further questions, the meeting moved to bonuses."

7. "Bonuses. Like last Xmas we are again awarding bonuses based on longevity and leadership. We are doing this because we have too many new workers that cannot yet qualify by more individual criteria such as we shall use next Xmas—individual productivity, value to company, commitment to job, ability to work with others, and demonstrated leadership capabilities."

"We feel strongly that bonuses should be kept private. It serves no one to flash the amount in your envelope and may even irritate other workers.

Certainly, this bonus amount is none of the public's business. For those of you under six months on the job, please use this money to stabilize your finances. For anyone more than six months with us, it is time to start a personal retirement account."

Amy took over, "when it comes time to retire, that 35% of your salary will only buy the essentials such as food and clothing. You need your own nest egg to properly provide for your retirement. So take your bonus, start a new bank account that generates interest, and leave it in the bank. At Xmas, you'll be able to add to it, and hopefully, every six months thereafter. On that note, we are passing out your envelope and please open it in private."

The Duo watched the group, everyone was opening their envelope careful enough not to show the amount to anyone. It was clear there was not a disappointed face in the crowd—smiles were the standard mixed with a lot of lipped Thank You's. With time gone by, Sam added some closing words. "Don't forget your ID cards if you show up here after hours, because you won't get in without it. Even if you take something from your own work area, you'll have to sign for it—as required by the security personnel. And last but not least, we have a vote count for the employee of the season. Oh my, we have a tie." After checking with Amy, Sam said, "each winner gets $200, and they are Ike Webb and Kent Knowles." The place erupted in laughter and applause as both recipients got up to collect their bank draft and certificate. "And that does it, have a pleasant vacation and see you at the double ring wedding."

*

The Duo treated the vacation as time away from the shop and all the business planning activities. They went to the theatre downtown, went fishing, skinny dipping at their favorite pool, went on long rides with picnics, and plenty of fancy restaurant stops for supper before the theatre.

Before they knew it, it was Wednesday, and time for a party. As promised, Sam kept his word, and both newlyweds got three nights and two full days at the better hotels in the city—of course separate hotels since a honeymoon was a private matter. The party was the best dancing the Duo did in a long time. Everyone danced as well, and it reflected a degree of stress-free behavior from those on vacation.

The Duo's last four days of vacation was finally spent with the special people in their lives: the

Barkers, the Holts, the Smiths, and the Whitacres (after their return from their honeymoon). The Duo treated and brought each couple to those French and Italian restaurants in the city, for an evening of catching up, laughter, and good food—of course it also included an evening in the theatre—exclusively the comedy theatre.

The last Sunday, after church, the Holts joined them for an afternoon of speed shooting at the local club, and a great time was had by all. It was that Sunday night that the Duo found themselves talking about work and planning for the future.

"You know Amy, when I was talking about converting to 45ACP I was at a loss for presenting a timeline for such a change. Do you think we could start working on that as the months go by?" "Sam, I've been working on that since January. Let me present two issues. First, we are building a massive escrow of prepaid 45ACP ammo. Ike is only taking $500 orders with free shipping for the new cartridge. Gun shop owners are ordering without second thoughts. We are accumulating over $100,000 a month, and doing a wire transfer to the parent Wells Fargo Bank in San Francisco for security against bank robberies. At your request, we don't keep more than $10,000 in operating funds at the local bank." "Ok, so how are we planning to satisfy those orders?"

"Yes, this is where I am prepared. In January we put out 68,000 rounds a day, that meant 1,360 fifty round ammo boxes. Because we weren't at full loaders, we were using our surplus cases to meet the orders. By June 1st, our orders were down to 40,000 rounds a day, or 800 ammo boxes a day. You were so busy, so I told Glen to keep a machine producing only 45ACP cases. So after he spent a week making 25,000 cases for Ira, he continued and made 75,000 cases for us for the remainder three weeks. And if we continue making that for the next seven months, we'll end up with +- a half million cases by Xmas."

Also, by Xmas, our 38 and 44 orders will be down to +-20-25,000 a day, and we'll be able to start producing more ACP cases." "So these statistics are all based on the six machines we now have?" "Yes, any machines from #7 to #12 is a different ball game and that would begin with the new workers by Xmas. We'll have all summer to buy these machines. Like you said at the meeting, one machine equals 5 men and six machines equal 30 new fabricators." "And that is why we are waiting for letters from E. Carruthers and W. Winthrop."

"Now, when do we start producing loaded 45ACP ammo to start filling those orders starting in Denver as promised?" "Well the answer is that we need to fill the 38 and 44 orders first, and then finish the day with 45ACP. It will be a gradual transfer to 45ACP ammo, and we'll have to work closely with Ann to make this happen. I can't predict how low our daily 38 and 44 orders will drop to, but I do predict that the downward trend will start next January as the upward production of 45ACP ammo will climb upwards."

"It looks like we may be selling 45ACP cases to Ira before we have a chance to start producing loaded 45ACP ammo." "Yes, it is very likely." "Well, let's get some sleep, we go back to work tomorrow, and we'll have an entire week of orders to process plus the daily new orders. It sounds like we'll both be as busy as a two-peckered owl again." "Maybe so, but for tonight, I'll deal with one of those, heh?" "Yes Ma'am."

*

Arriving first at the shop, as usual, the Duo knew there was something different other than the ceiling and ventilation fans. The surplus of all loading components had significantly increased.

The Duo decided to say nothing till someone fessed up. The crew arrived and it was Kent who finally addressed the situation. "Luke, I count about 40 new crates of supplies. Where did they come from with the shop closed for business?" "Well, I went to the railroad yard on Friday and found the railroad was holding our supplies in one boxcar—which was packed full. They agreed to bring it to our dock on Saturday if I could find two RR men to unload the boxcar. Well, I offered some cold cash, and got two men on my first inquiry—these were good men with large families that needed the extra income. Well they worked hard all day, placed each of the forty 300-pound crates where I wanted them, and the job got done. Had to do it, we just didn't have the time to do the extra work this week."

The Duo and half the staff were listening to all this, when Sam asked, "how much did you pay these men?" "$20 each, and they earned every penny!" "That was a nice pay, and I presume you paid them out of your pocket." "Of course, that was part of my job." "Well, you know where the petty cash box is, so pay yourself back and give yourself twice the salary you gave those men, heh? And I saw that the loaders all have their components to start working this morning—I suppose your guardian angel did all that prep work as well?" "Just used the time between crates."

After the foremen got the workers assigned or back at their loading bench, the Duo started their day by opening the mail. It was one order after another and large amounts in telegraph vouchers or bank drafts.

Amy was busy entering the orders in the ledger when Sam, who was opening the bills and general mail, came up to a letter from W. Winthrop and one from E. Caruthers. Sam started with Wendell's letter.

> *Dear Sam and Amy,*
>
> *"As you may recall, the 8-month program was once appropriate for this college, but times are changing. There is a renewed interest in a trade's education, and we now have two 6-month sessions per year at the new cost of $1,000 per session for tuition, books, and room & board. The sessions are more intensive with daily evening classes or labs, as well as all day Saturday labs or private projects."*

"Now more appropriate to your needs, some word has gotten around about your company, wages, benefits, and working women in the shop. There is a lot interest these days in brass cartridge fabrication because of the shooting sports that are developing and companies like yours. It's unbelievable, but I have 25 students who have registered brass fabrication as their major. Of those 25, twenty have expressed a firm interest in applying for work in your shop—those 20 applications are enclosed. Of the twenty, 2 are married with children, plus 12 others are also financially able to pay the $1,000 registration fee, and 6 are short of funds and plan to do 'work study.' With the intensive schedule, there is no time for 'work study,' so I introduced these six to your offer. All six are impressive young students, and all six signed the 18-month agreement. After leaving these six at least $50 for personal needs, your contribution

would come to +-$2,400 to finalize this contract."

"It is of note that none of these 20 students need to visit your shop and that is why the applications are all enclosed. And so in short, you have 20 workers who will be trained by Xmas. These are individuals of good stock with strong work ethics—you will be pleased. I may also add that I have been working in conjunction with Elroy Caruthers who also has changed his sessions to 6 months. He has some students that will sign up with you, but wait for specifics till you get his letter."

"As always, have a good summer and one day I will show up to visit this shop that everyone is talking about."
Your truly, Wendell.

Sam then gave Amy the letter to read as he read the letter from E. Caruthers. Handing the second letter for Amy to read, the Duo finally looked at each other as Amy said, "seems to me that the die is cast." Sam turned around and asked for Irene.

"Irene, things are changing. We need six full 5-man fabricating machines. So contact Big Blu and see if you can get a discount on six machines in 45ACP, then order them no matter what the cost. We want them installed anytime, but no later than December 1st. Also notify Ira Winchester and ask if there is a limit in the number of 45ACP casings we send them each month. Then order a dozen more 45ACP loading dies from Lionel Lofton."

"As you can see, the time we convert to 45ACP is soon approaching, so push hard to build our surplus of loading components for this new caliber as well as keep building our surplus of 45 caliber brass buds. And last of all, read these two letters and send Wendell $2,400 and Elroy $1,500 as well as mail these signed contracts back to them."

"So now Amy, we fill out all these 38 and 44 orders, and start the transitioning period to 45ACP brass cartridge fabrication, and to loading this caliber in anticipation of the semi-automatic pistol coming on the market. And let's not forget we have a man on the road that is still selling our press, and taking large orders of prepaid 45ACP ammo."

"Yes, and we now have a large Wells Fargo bank account in San Francisco, plus an escrow account in the Texas Community Bank in Houston, as well as the parent First National Bank in Denver. These three parent banks have high security and are all accessed thru our local banks in Dallas. Like our component suppliers, we no longer put all our eggs in one basket, heh?"

***

CHAPTER 8

Transitioning to 45ACP

The next six months turned out to be some routine days filled with continuous work for everyone. The one person that dictated the days activities was Luke. He had devised a system that utilized the previous day's orders as compared to the previous arrangement of loaders for each caliber. So every morning he would tell Ann that he needed so many of loaders for all five categories—38 Target, 38 Hot, 44 Target, 44 Hot, and 45ACP Hot. Along with this Glen was also advised how many machines had to be assigned to 38, 44, or 45ACP. As much as the Duo tried to understand his system, they could not make any sense out of it. All they knew was that it worked, and both Ann and Glen were happy to comply with the day's orders—for the ends justified the means in their book.

The Duo carefully reviewed the ledger at the end of each month. It was clear that a surplus was slowly building of 45ACP casings as well as a surplus of loaded ammo that was processed and stored for now. Of the most importance, this slow building of 45ACP surplus was not interfering with putting out the 38 and 44 orders that came in each day. But what it did mean was that the surplus casings for 38s and 44s was quickly disappearing—for this reason, the Duo decided to have a meeting with their man on the road—Ike Webb.

"Well here we are, November is just around the bend, and we have to decide whether to let orders for 38s and 44s plateau below 20,000 rounds a day, or add some new marketing ploy to increase the orders. In the past, your knowledge and current events from the hundreds of gun shops you see each month has been valuable, and even lifesaving in making plans for this shop. So we'd appreciate your thought on this issue." "Before I present my alternative argument, would you present the plan for increasing orders?"

Sam looked at Amy who took the lead, "like when we went to Denver, the only way to increase orders is to add new customers. Now Texas has a population of 3 million, and there is another state that has the same population—Missouri next door. St. Louis MO has a population of 600,000 people and is only 600 miles from Dallas. Also, Kansas City MO has a population of 175,000 and is 500 miles from Dallas—a shade closer than Denver was with a much smaller population." Sam then added, "with your past performance, there are +- 500-gun shops between these two cities, and at 4 visits per day, we suspect you can see all these gun shops in the next 6 months. (500 ÷ 4 = 125 workdays which is +- 25 weeks)

"Of course, I can do this. But before you decide, let me present a new and different approach based on my past experience in loading ammo and visiting hundreds of gun shops. Let's start with a reality check; let's assume those 30 college boys are here, and you have 12 five-man machines in full operation."

"You now have 36 loaders who are each producing 2,500 rounds a day. That is an amazing 90,000 rounds a day, or 450,000 rounds a week. Now that requires 90,000 new fabricated casings each day. Well your fabrication production per five-man machine is now up to 5,500 a day. So 12 machines can put out 66,000 new casings a day." Ike stopped for effect and then added, "so where will you get these 24,000 casings, you're short of each day once your surplus is exhausted—which I suspect is very soon, heh?"

The Duo went silent, when Sam finally spoke, "we need those extra 24,000 cases each day just to keep the loaders working. I guess we'll have to offer a second shift Monday and Wednesday night, or a full shift on Saturday—all on volunteer time and a half. Or in June we add more fabrication machines and hire more college graduates." "Hu-uhm, does it ever stop, and when do you grow beyond efficiency and profitability?"

Amy, with a smile, adds, "I know your mind works like a lawyer for you never ask a question or present a problem without having an answer, so out with it, what is the alternative? We like the size of our company and don't really want to ever expand again."

"Eliminate the need to fabricate 20,000, 38/44 casings, each day!" "But Ike, we spent the past two years building this clientele, and we don't want to close their business, it isn't right!" "I absolutely feel you must continue filling their order, it's just that you need another cheap source of 38 and 44 casings." "And where do we get them?" "You buy 'once fired brass' of smokeless casings at a half penny a piece."

"WHAAAAAT, tells us more." "Ever since I took this job, I've been selling your 38 and 44 smokeless ammo, but have asked the gun shop owners to save used, or once fired brass, as long as they are not the damaged cases from black powder. I've even told them to pay a quarter of a penny a piece and eventually they will double their money. Now, I will guess that you have a couple million cases right here in Dallas's 21- gun shops and three speed shooting clubs. I bet you that if I take off with a freighter that I'll be back today with all the 'once fired brass' in this town."

"Assuming that is possible, and we notify all our Texas customers that we are paying a half penny per case plus paying the shipping, we still need to clean the cases and polish them—and how do we do that with millions to process?" Amy quickly added, "and why do I know that you've already solved that problem?" "Well, it so happens that I have. I've been working with Bert Holiday for weeks. After checking the literature in the library, we have devised a 4 gallon electrically powered rotary tumbler. You add 1/3 with brass cartridges,1/3 with white beach sand used in kid's sand boxes, and leave 1/3 of air space. Then place the barrel on a 30-degree rotating base and let the brass tumble for an hour. It will come out looking like new. As long as the loaders check their case before placing it on the press, they can discard the occasional ruined case from BP, someone stepping on a case, and other cosmetic defects. The final result will be a new round that looks like new—the case cost you a half penny, and your brass fabricators will now be free to make all 45ACP cases, with or without, extra shifts at time and a half."

Sam was totally flabbergasted and spent a few minutes before speaking. "I admit, it is a perfect alternative, but it's going to take some time to get this all organized and ready to clean its first batch of cases." "No Sam, do the following:

1. Send Cyrus to Asa's to pick up the three reserved bags of white beach sand—and leave the other ten bags till we need them.
2. On his way back to the shop, have him stop at my house and pick up the three powered rotary tumblers that Bert built for you.
3. Miss Amy, start typing a notice to all Texas gun shops that you are buying 'once fired brass' at a half penny a piece plus paying for the shipping if packed in 50-pound fixed rate boxes that hold +- 4,000 cases per box

(38s weigh 9 pounds per 1000 cases, and 44s weigh 13 pounds per 1000 cases). Send this notice only to Texas shops to save on shipping.

4. As you are typing, have Luke set up the printing type.

5. Send Irene to the telegraph office and send a notice to all gun shops in the two nearest large centers—Fort Worth and Houston. That way, when the Dallas supply is exhausted, these two communities will be sending their surplus. Be careful to remind everyone that the 38s are not to be mixed with the 44s— they must be kept separate.

6. I will go find a freighter and be back with every 'once fired 38 and 44 brass' in town— of which I estimated to be a couple million."

"Then by tonight, we'll have the 20,000 cases needed to fill tomorrow's orders."

*

By noon, Ike arrived at the warehouse doors with two full loaded wagons. Each 5-gallon pail weighed +-75 pounds and had roughly 6,000 cases per pail. With the help from Luke, Kent, Sam, Ike and two freighters the group had all 300 pails stored in the warehouse. Next to the outside warehouse doors, Sam had set up a work bench where the three rotary tumblers will do their job—and keep the noise of tumbling brass away from the loaders.

Amy was watching and computed 300 pails of 6,000 casings per pail meant 1.8 million casings. At a half penny each, that meant $9,000. What the Duo did not realize was how the gun shops would get paid. When asked, Ike said, "I gave them a receipt for the exact weight of each pail. When the gun shop places their next order, you will give them their credit if the gun shop owner didn't already deduct it from his payment—as I've encouraged them to do. That way, there is no cash outlay on your part, and instead it is a working account credit." "Excellent."

So, the boys got a quick "how to" course on how to load this rotating barrel. "You weigh out 25 pounds of cases, either 38s or 44s, and add 25 pounds of white sand. Close the cover, place on its base, turn the power on, and walk away. Come back in one hour and the cases are ready for the loaders. To get 20,000 cases cleaned up, you'll probably need four batches over a half day of rotating time. The total labor time is probably a half hour a day for Kent, Luke, or you Sam. Or you could get Ann's assistant, Craig Dufield, to add this to his duties."

The Duo finally admitted that Ike saved the day, and prevented more expansion that was not a popular solution. Ike finally admitted, "I did all this so you could now officially admit that today, this shop is fabricating only 45ACP casings." "We agree, and are happy to see this day come. Now it's compensation time. We owe you for hours of planning, time spent at the carpentry shop, untold expenses, three automated rotating cleaners, and arranging an equitable payment for the 'once fired brass.'"

Ike put his hands up in the classic "stop" formation. "It seems, one day I came home and found someone had paid my mortgage. Then I went to my first of your 6-month meeting and came home with a bunch of money. Then I went to the last pre vacation meeting and again came home with more money and a life insurance benefit. Am I making myself clear. I finally got to experience some payback by looking out for this company's stability and welfare—and I feel 'real good.' We're square, heh?" Sam looked at Amy, and with the nod, she stepped up to Ike and gave him a hug as she whispered, "Thank You for looking out for us, for we never saw this coming. Now that you enlightened us, it is so clear and obvious. Most important, we don't have to expand again."

*

That night at home, the Duo sat in their parlor, and brought up the subject of how to proceed for the next 50 days to the holidays when the 30 new fabricators would arrive. They both realized that the real issue was whether to start pushing the fabrication of 45ACP to build a surplus, and to load the 38 and 44's nonstop to use the 'once fired brass' to also create an inventory surplus OR to continue Luke's mixed approach which is what got them to this point since the July vacation. The Duo discussed the pros and cons for an hour when Amy said, "I know that it boils down to 'six of one and half a dozen of the other,' but I like to build an inventory while we meet our commitments."

"So what you're saying, have the loaders load 38s and 44s 'once fired brass,' straight to when the college boys arrive—to meet the daily orders and build a surplus inventory of loaded rounds. At the same time, let the six fabricating teams fabricate 45ACP cases uninterrupted." "Yes, and I would offer them any night or Saturday, a 7-hour second shift, whenever they have 5 men willing to work 5-12 midnight or the seven hours on Saturday. That way, no one is pushing the men who don't want the extra work, and allows the younger crowd to make the extra money at time and a half for a shorter 7-hour second shift or a Saturday day."

Sam then presented Amy with another change. "In preparing for the big transfer to loading 45ACP in January, Craig Dufield was already setting the 45ACP dies on the extra tool heads, but pointed out that the shell-plates had to be changed to handle the new casing. Neil had been notified, and had already started making 36 new shell-plates." Amy then asked, "what about the large pistol priming system, don't we need 36 of them?" "Yes, but Neil had made plenty of those in anticipation to selling them?" "Neil had already made a bunch of them to sell to the press owners—which never happened. For the same reason, with a surplus of unsold powder measures, Sam is attaching them to the tool head for ACP loading." "So the surplus priming system and powder measures will go to good use."

"Well we are 50 workdays away to the holidays and the 6 teams of fabricators should make a minimum of 33,000 cases a day and for 50 days will end up with 1.65 million 45ACP casings—which is the inventory we need to start loading the new caliber." "Plus more if they work overtime."

"In the same light, the loaders will load 90,000 rounds a day of 38s or 44s. Over the next 50 days that comes to a whopping 4.5 million rounds. Of that, at 20,000 a day to fill orders, then in 50 days we'll use up 1 million and thereby leaving 3.5 million in reserve for filling out orders next year—and that comes to 175 days without having to load any 38 or 44 casings."

The next day, the Duo had a quick meeting with the foremen to inform them of the changes that needed implementation. Once the foremen were at their stations, Sam went in the warehouse and filled the three tumblers with sand and casings. It became an hourly ritual which ended with a total of 6,000 clean and polished casings per hour, or a total of 48,000 cases per day. After a full day of this work, Sam decided that this was a fulltime job. The polished brass would have to be weighed to fill a 300-pound crate. By sticking to 300 pounds per crate, the 38s would add up to +-33,000 casings, and the 44s would add up to +-23,000 cases.

Sam went to see Amy, "when we hired those last two loaders, who how many did we reserve for future employment?" "Six, four women and two men." "How old are the men?" "25 and 50. The older gentleman is a brother to one of our loaders." "Good, I'll send Cyrus to pick him up if still available and we're going to make him the brass processing agent before we get flooded with casings."

That afternoon, Cyrus arrived with Walt Denison. "Thank you for coming in. I would like to offer you a job that is a new position in the shop. I recall our training you to load ammo, and you will eventually be moved to that section, but now we need someone to clean and polish 'once fired brass' coming in from the many Texas gun shops. Are you interested?" "Absolutely, I'll do any job!" "Fine, then let me show you what you'll need to do."

"First you load the rotating tumblers.....................Then after an hour you unload them. The sand and cartridge mixture is put in this 5/16 sifter and rotated between this scoop and the sifter a half dozen times till the sand is in the sifter bucket. Then the 25 pounds of brass cartridges is added to the 300-pound crate—one for the 38s and one for the 44s. Then you refill the tumbler and repeat every hour. In a day's time you will process up to 48,000 casings."

"So far so good, and what do I do when I have to wait an hour to process the next batch?" "Come with me, you need to learn how to handle a 300-pound electric hydraulic lift to stack these 300-pound crates three crates high." On their way to the loading/receiving area, Sam grabbed both Kent and Luke. Before long, Kent had Walt handling the lift like an expert. Walt brought his first 300-pound crate to his processing area not knowing what was in the crate.

Opening the crate were six 50-pound fixed rate boxes from two gun shops. "Now you enter in this ledger the name of the gun shop and its address with the number of FR-50/38, and of FR-50/44 boxes received. Then you place the box of 38s on this pallet, and the 44s on that pallet, and all stacked three box high, only to prevent the cardboard from collapsing. Every day, there will be a freight delivery by train boxcar and your second job is to pick them up and place them where they belong— and every one of those FR-50 boxes will need to be processed for months to come." "Anything else I need to do?"

"Yes, every afternoon, check with Ann, for the exact number of 38 and 44 loaders. Then fill these 36 containers with 30 pounds of processed brass (that's +- 2,500 casings) to match the type of loader on the floor. At 4PM, use one of these expediting wagons and deliver the containers to each loading bench, bringing back the empty container to your bench for tomorrow's use. 4PM is the time loaders stop loading, and pump primers for tomorrow." "What do I do if the cartridge container is not empty?" "Add the leftovers to your full container and gather the now empty ones, heh."

So today, I'm going to work with you, but tomorrow you're on your own. After a few days, I'll come and see how things are going, and see if we need to modify this job. Just for the record, this end of day cartridge distribution used to be Kent's duty, so he'll be happy to see you do it."

Four days later, Sam came to see how Walt was doing. "I'm doing well and feel comfortable doing this job, but there is one problem." "And that is?" "Everyone is always working, and I sit on my duff half of the afternoons. It is not right, and I need more things to do." "Well, you're the first to complain that you are underworked, but I understand. So, what do you think we should do differently?"

"Double the number of tumblers or let me be the backup loader. Yesterday, Ann had a sick lady loader, and her bench stayed empty all day."

"Which choice do you prefer?" "How about both. When Ann doesn't need a replacement loader, I will process brass at twice the speed and keep busy. In four days, look at the millions of brass pieces in those FR-50 boxes." "I agree, so I'll call Bert Holiday and order three more tumblers. Plus, Ann will now know to call on you when a substitute loader is needed. Also, when the white sand gets grey and lumpy, and the brass is no longer shiny, change the sand—irrelevant of the total tumbling days. What we want is a shiny casing that looks like new."

Over the next weeks, Ann started to have ladies absent for one to three days at a time. It was clear that these were the newlyweds from last summer, and morning sickness was getting to be a problem. It was Irene who passed the message around that pregnant gals should have a half dozen soda crackers at their bedside. They needed to eat them and drink some water before visiting the water closet—an old tried and true method to control morning sickness.

During this time, Walt was working full time as a loader, and the other five workers on reserve all got to start working and get enrolled in the employee benefits—if they worked, they got paid, but if they didn't work, they did not get paid but still had the same benefits. They were now considered the substitute staff with full benefits. As people quit, died, retired, or left town, these substitute staff would all eventually become full time employees.

The influx of 'once fired brass' was getting out of hand. When the Duo along with Walt estimated that they had approximately 20 million 38/44 casings on hand, and several millions more could arrive. At Walt's rate of polishing 85,000 cases a day, it would take him +- 240 days to do the job. Amy typed a memo putting an end to buying 'once fired brass' till further notice—100-gun shops were immediately notified by telegram, and the balance by postal service. Gun shops were encouraged to keep collecting them because they would soon be able to buy smokeless powder and then convert their BP presses to smokeless reloading.

What they didn't know was that Ike Webb had purchased the patent on these tumblers from Bert Holiday, and would sell them in conjunction with Holiday Construction to all of TEXAS LOAD'S customers. Their moto became "once fired brass looks like new with our tumblers." By the time they started selling tumblers, Bert got 1/3 for cost of materials, and 1/3 for labor. The profit section got spread among three individuals since Ike worked for TEXAS LOAD. Of the 33%, Bert got 13%, Ike got 10%, and the Duo got 10% for adding it to their RED BULLET-IN and certifying it as a working unit that cleaned and polished 'once fired brass.'

*

The next weeks seemed to go smoothly. The fabricators were making 45ACP casings, the loaders were making 38 and 44 ammo to cover the 20,000 rounds ordered each day, and was building a surplus of the same loaded ammo for the future. The machinists were busy making accessory parts for the press frames, as Irene was shipping out the finished product to the prepaid customers.

Ike was still busy taking prepaid orders for 45ACP. Amy had kept tract of each prepaid order as they came in. Ike was now carrying a note pad with all prepaid orders that were taken in proper order—from first to current order. So when Ike accepted a prepaid order, the buyer was given a sequential number as the gun shop was added to the note pad. That simple method prevented owners from trying to jump the line. It was Ike's selling line—"even if low on this list, you're still a preferred customer. It is a heck better than not being on it where you would get nothing for many months if not years."

Week after week, the brass fabricators would usually have two evening 7-hour shifts of fabricating the new casings, as well as a full 7-hour shift on Saturday. The current fabricators knew that 30 fabricators were arriving after Xmas, and overtime could likely disappear. The result was 80% overall attendance with overtime hours. It was Amy who came down with an amazing statistic. "For eight weeks before Xmas, the six fully staffed machines made: 5,500 pieces a day per machine X 6 machines = 33,000 per day X 5-day week = 165,000 pieces a week X 8 weeks = 1.32 million. Now add three extra day shifts per week and you have a total of 24 extra shifts in 8 weeks. Assuming each shift can produce 80% of 33,000 pieces or 26,400 pieces per shift X 24 extra shifts = 634,000 extra cases. Add this to 1.32 million and you have 1.95 million pieces fabricated. This serves as the inventory surplus, minus the monthly allotment of 25,000 cases sent to Winchester."

With the weeks gone by, the Duo decided to have the yearly meeting before the Xmas weekend since Xmas was on a Friday. So the day started with payday at 10AM on Thursday morning, followed by a social hour, with lunch being the end of year full dinner, followed by the afternoon meeting. This time, the wives, significant others, or future partners being courted, were invited to the entire day's event.

In anticipation of the yearly meeting, the foremen had had a week to fill out their individual assessments of each worker in his or her section. Ann had 36 loaders, Neil had two, Titus and Jim Whitefield, the new college boy machinist. Glen had 35 fabricators, Luke had Kent and Walt. Ida had Lucille, Edna, and Hans. Irene had Cyrus and Ike. The Duo had the six foremen to consider but not evaluate like the workers were scrutinized.

The criteria these foremen had to follow included:

1. Individual productivity.
2. Essential value to company.
3. Commitment to job.
4. Willingness to do extra work when needed.
5. Demonstrated leadership capabilities.

Foreman's negative comments: _____

The Duo explained that #1-5 each needed a rating of 1 to 3 points. Most good workers would get at least 2 points per category—which meant a total of 10 points (at $20 a point) that meant a bonus of $200. Those with the 1-point award would be a sign for an area to improve—for every worker would receive his or her assessment card with the bonus. Of note, and negative comments was a real flag for the worker, since it also meant a $40 deduction off their bonus. For the record, a duplicated assessment card was left in the worker's file.

Later that evening, as the Duo was writing out the bonus bank drafts, they commented on the usual reasons for a foreman's negative comment.

- Always 20 minutes late to arrive and start work.
- Occasionally falls asleep on job.
- Not sociable with other workers.
- Needs to bathe more and control BO.
- Tends to drag out breaks to finish their smokes.
- Not pleasant to expediters—they claim that they either are too early or late with components and supplies.
- Abandons horse at barn without taking care of it—forcing Cyrus to take care of the animal.

*

The meeting day was going well with the beer and wine social hour. The Duo commented how the wives and significant others added to the crowd. Darcy had outdone herself with a choice of beef stew or chicken fricassee, fresh bread, and a dessert of bread pudding and coffee. Eventually, the highlight of the day had arrived.

"Welcome to the second annual meeting. Next week, we'll be welcoming another 30 fabricators to make our plant total of 115 workers—and we are not expanding or adding more workers." *Laughter and applause.*

"That means that starting Jan 1ˢᵗ, we will be a plant with one goal, that of fabricating and loading 45ACP ammo. We will start fulfilling our pre-paid orders to Colorado and New Mexico and in a week, we'll be filling the orders for Dallas, Fort Worth and Houston in the order that Ike accepted the orders. Then, the rest of Texas gun shops will follow."

"During this time, the processing staff will also fill out the daily orders for 38 and 44 ammo, but this will not affect the fabricators and loaders, since we have six months' worth of loaded ammo boxes in storage. Also concurrently, Neil and the machinists will be making scales and powder measures to sell to the press owners as they convert their BP press to loading the now available smokeless powder."

"Now I know that some of you worry about the rumors that this semi-automatic pistol is just an idea, and years away for reality—if it is really true. Well, Amy and I have had a Colt pistol in hand and fired several magazine. I can tell you; this will happen. For the next 100+ years, the semi-automatic pistol will dominate the handgun market."

Amy then added, "this pistol is the future of the shooting sports, will be powerful to stop a human opponent, put down any predator in Texas, will become the lawman's side arm, and the military will soon accept it as the standard soldier's side arm. In short, it will replace the Peacemaker and the new double action revolvers on the market."

Sam took over. "I have been told by Alden Pickett, Colt's regional distributor, that the pistol will be in Texas gun shops by early summer. We also have 100% support from Lionel Lofton of the Houston Foundry, and of Ira Winchester, that converting our plant to the 45ACP cartridge is the only guarantee for the survival of this factory and your jobs. In other words, either we follow the trend, or we'll go bankrupt. So, those are our thoughts and we're sticking to them. On Sunday afternoon six of us, Amy and I, Neil and Ann, and Glen and Irene, will set all 36 presses to the new 45ACP caliber so the loaders can start loading the new rounds on arrival to work on Monday. It is also of note that in the past 50 days, our fabricators produced an inventory of 1.9 million 45ACP cases, so we are ready. The stats show that 36 loaders will produce 90,000 loaded rounds a day, while the 12 fabricating machines will produce 66,000 new casings per day. So, there will be overtime fabricating offered in the future." *More applause and signs of approval on workers' faces.*

"Next on my agenda, we have two workers whose suggestions made them qualified for the $25 award. Craig Dufield for installing the 45ACP loading dies to the extra toolheads before the final setting of the powder measure on Sunday. The other is to Elmer Whitacre, for preheating the brass bud with an electric heat gun before starting the drawing process. This has increased the machine's daily production from 5,000 to 5,500." *Plenty of applause, guffaws, and whistles.*

"FYI, the warehouse is 70% full, the back of the loading A-Wing is 50% full of bullets, and the old steel room and storage room are still empty, and will remain empty till a good use for them is found.

And that takes care of my informative agenda. Now the monetary section."

Amy took over, "in the past we've added employee benefits, and these will remain the same for the next year." *Much applause.* This year, Sam and I feel that a raise is in order. Now keep in mind that a raise is in perpetuity whereas bonuses vary year to year or can even be absent when times are tough—but raises are never taken back. With this in mind, we are placing an across the board raise increase of 50 cents a day, which comes to an extra $125 a year for every worker (there are +-250 workdays a year)." *More prolonged and loud applause with whistles.*

"Finally, we come to bonuses. You all know we've had a good profitable year, and we will again share some of the profits with you. This year, the size of your bonus is not based on longevity with TEXAS LOAD. It is based on personal issues as graded by your foreman and approved by Amy and me. Everyone will have a score card of points with your envelope, plus a copy in your file, that shows how we arrived at your bonus. It will also show where improvements can occur in the future, and any negative comments must be corrected if you plan to stay with us. So, don't go home grumbling at your foreman. Instead, try to improve. I may add that the majority of our workers had a positive report."

"Like last June, please keep your bonus amount private, and we hope you can put it in your retirement account." The workers pocketed their envelopes, as they took their departure, to open them in private.

***

CHAPTER 9

Gearing up for the 45ACP

It was now Christmas Eve and Sam had put off going to the city to get presents for the Barkers, Whitacres, Smiths, and Holts. This year it was not simple to buy for these four couples that had everything and needed nothing. It was Amy who had gone to Alden Pickett and got into an agreement with him to guarantee five boxes of 45 ACP ammo (at $5 a box) to any gun shop that buys a Colt semi-automatic pistol. For her part, she paid $500 for ten brand new pistols out of the box (including one for Sam and one for her). Along with the pistol, each recipient also received, a belted holster, two extra magazines, two magazine holders (of course for another $200), and five boxes of ammo. In the future, she figured that if they were all going to make casings and load the ammo, that they could each use free ammo from the shop and enjoy shooting this firearm. When Amy told Sam what she had done, not mentioning the two extra pistols for her and Sam, he was thrilled. He added, "well that simplifies our shopping, we're down to you and me. So what do you want for Xmas?"

"I want something I've wanted all my life—a baby!" Sam looked dumbstruck and obfuscated. Amy continued, "we've put off some crucial loving days because of safe sex that we practiced for the past three years. I want to enjoy you 100% of the time and 100% of each day. Our business is now stable and what we produce now will probably be what we'll produce in five years. If I can't do my job, I'll hire someone to help me and take over when I take my maternity leave. So what say you— we know friends can be lovers, but can friends become parents and raise a family."

"Oh my gosh, I am so ready to be a parent. But as a Xmas present, I look forward to enjoying our mutual ecstasy—TOGETHER from now on. Sam grabbed Amy and as they were in a passionate embrace, Sam pulled a HIP. Amy quickly responded with, "I want my present, NOW!"

After a memorable Xmas Eve, the Duo had their light breakfast of toast, peanut spread, and coffee.

Lingering till about 9AM, they were finally on their way to the Whitacres for the traditional family Xmas gathering, dinner, and the tree's opening. Stopping on their way to the Holts and the Smiths, to deliver their Xmas presents, they still managed to arrive at their father's house on time.

As usual, it was a pleasant social gathering and a fantastic turkey dinner. When it came time to open the presents, Amy distributed ten small boxes— the magazine holders (with the questioning look). Then another small box—the two extra magazines (the look of recognition). Then a larger box—the belt and holster (the look of satisfaction). And finally the largest box—the Colt semi-automatic pistol (the look of total awe). Finally it was Luke who said, "how on earth did you ever arrange to get these before their official introduction?" "Not a problem, from the man who is hoarding about 3,000 of them in a secure warehouse—without a single box of ammo. I made him an offer he could not refuse! Heh?"

After the Duo opened their presents, it was Ida who said, "well I don't know about you all, but Luke and I are going to the range to try these pistols out." As it was clear that everyone was going along, Sam answered, "and we are going with you to make sure you handle these new firearms properly and safely." "Then in that case, here is yours Sam and this one is mine, heh?" "Why of course dear. It's nice to see you want to play too."

*

The next week was going well with the loaders changing calibers. The loaders who had been loading 38 special took a bit longer to get use to the larger and shorter casing as well as changing to large pistol primers. But by Wednesday, they all mastered the change and were all putting out their 2,500 loaded rounds a day.

The same Wednesday was the day that all 30 new fabricators were expected to arrive from El Paso and Houston. The Duo was at the Union Pacific terminal at 11AM. To their surprise, both trains were delayed. The El Paso train was diverted away from going to Midland because a bridge was out, and ended up also diverted from the alternative Austin route because of tracks being washed out. So the El Paso train was diverted to Houston. The trains departure from Houston now had all 30 college boys heading to Dallas, and expected to arrive by 1PM. To compensate the passengers for all the diversions and delays, all were given a full dinner in the dining car. The Duo had a two hour wait, so they decided to have a prolonged dinner at Darcy's as well as play hooky from work.

The conversation at dinner turned to hiring help for Amy. Amy admitted that she wanted a recent college graduate in the commercial field. Sam added, "oh no, not another 19-year-old gal of marrying age. What is the public going to think of us?" "I don't care, I want someone who can be molded to this job, not someone opinionated about their years of old ways." "Ok, but before we advertise in the newspaper, let's pass the word around amongst our workers. We may just have a daughter or grand-daughter who was a holiday graduate in town and looking for a job." "Wow, that's a fantastic idea, I like the notion that we always go for internal replacements before going outside the shop."

It was now time to head to the RR terminal and wait for the train from Houston. Standing on the platform, Amy was holding a TEXAS LOAD sign. Throngs of people were exiting off 4 packed passenger cars. Slowly, the new fabricators were gathering around Amy. Sam finally said, "I count 12 of you, where are the other 18?" A spokesman said, "oh 16 went in the terminal to use the water closet. All of a sudden, one man said, "here they come." Sam and Amy turned around as Sam just about dislocated his lower jaw, and Amy broke out in laughter as she managed to add, "boy, the whole town will now believe we run a 'mate' matching shop."

A spokeswoman stepped up with Sam still frozen in shock. "Oh, oh. Something tells me that Mister Caruthers and Professor Winthrop did not tell you that half the fabricators were women who wanted to move to Dallas because of your reputation." Amy stopped laughing enough to ask, "and what reputation is that?" "That you provide excellent wages, incredible security benefits, and an integrated shop of men and women." Sam finally added, "yes, that is all true, but can you ladies put out new casings as well as men?"

The original spokesman stepped up and took the spokeswoman's hand and said, "I can personally vouch for these ladies, because they can multitask better than men can, they are a bit more productive." Some time passed as the spokeswoman decided to speak. "Sorry you were not informed, so we can all get back on the train and go back to the college for an alternative placement. The only problem is that some of the ladies accepted your contractual arrangement of tuition for guaranteed months of service. So, how do we repay you?"

Amy looked at Sam, and without a word being spoken, Sam took the lead. "Ladies, other than the surprise, since you are college trained fabricators, we would be happy to accept you and offer you a fulltime job, and a heck of a batch of eligible men. Welcome to TEXAS LOAD. The platform erupted in joyous applause as Amy spotted two couples kissing—as she placed their faces in her memory banks.

The last two fabricators were married men with wives and children. They then arrived with crates of baggage which the Duo was ready to receive in their buckboard. It was Amy who said, "we will deliver the families to their apartments, and the two men will come back with us. We will then all walk to the shop to introduce you to our workers and give you a tour of your future place of work."

Arriving at the shop, the group was swung into A-Wing where they met the 36 loaders, and introduced to Ann and craig Dufield at the control desk. Ann gave a quick demo how the ammo was created. Then a quick detour to the new C-Wing warehouse which also included Walt Denison busy with his tumblers—and another demo was included. Heading to the new B-Wing, they had to make a detour to avoid Kent riding his hydraulic loader with a full load heading to the warehouse— as Kent smiled and waved at the new batch of mostly women.

The group experienced their first 'shock and awe' as they stood in the archway to B-Wing. With all eyes fixed on the left side of the wing, there stood 30 men operating six 5-man machines, and a second row of six machines totally unmanned and sitting idle. It was clear that those idle machines would be their work area. Afterwards, the tour included Irene's press processing room and Neil's machining area. The last area on their tour was Ida's processing tables.

Sam then announced, "we have a break coming up. So mingle with the workers and get to know them over fresh lemonade. Afterwards, we will gather in the lunchroom to assign you your living quarters." As the break bell sounded, the mingling was between the young workers, so with things going well, the Duo extended the break till all the lemonade was gone.

Sam started with the men, "we have 14 men and 10 will be assigned to a boarding house with three meals a day and laundry service. So pair up with a buddy and step up for your new house's name and address."

Next Sam said that the two men with families were already assigned their apartments. Last, the two men with a significant other would be handled by Amy."

As Amy took over, "we have two men who have apparently paired up with a classmate. Do you ladies agree?" With a nod and a smile, Amy said, "we'll find you both a small economical apartment, and till then we'll house you in one of our chosen hotels as couples for your privacy."

"Now we have 14 ladies that need placement. Our plan is to find you all a boarding house with meals and laundry like we did with the men—but for ladies. It may take us a few days and till then, you will all be placed in hotels—but three to a room. Your meals will be paid for when any of you are being temporarily housed in the hotel—but only in the hotel's restaurant."

Sam finished the meeting as he passed everyone five $20 bills in US currency. This money is actually your 'sign on' bonus. Use it to get yourselves settled down. If you decide to buy new clothes, remember that your 'top' is a company shirt with a logo and free laundry. This being Wednesday, we'll have you settled in your new homes by the weekend. So for now, here are the ladies' hotel assignments. We'll plan to meet with the ladies tomorrow night with the boarding house assignments—we'll see you in the hotel restaurant after your supper."

The next day Sam started the day announcing that they were opening a new job to help Amy addressing orders and do office work. It was Vern from the old machinists' essential workers that spoke up. "Sam, my grand-daughter Samantha Bishop just got home Xmas Eve. She graduated from Houston in the commercial department, and is looking for a job. She is a pleasant gal, looks good, and smart as a whip. I think she would be a perfect match for Amy." Amy added, "great, ask her to meet me here at 4PM today for an interview."

Meanwhile, Amy and Irene took off with Cyrus to find housing for two couples and 14 single gals. It took all day, but by 3PM they had found all the necessary housing. Amy knew she had an interview waiting, so proceeded to the shop. When she got there, Sam greeted her with a smile and introduced Samantha to Amy. "Samantha arrived early, and Vern and I just gave her a tour of the shop, so she's all yours now."

Amy and Samantha went thru the basics of employment and benefits. Then things got personal. Amy admitted she was hoping to become pregnant soon, and Samantha would need to take over the office and processing job. Samantha admitted that she wanted to find a job with long term potential, and was pleased to work with so many men. She was hoping to find someone in this shop so they could continue working here as a married couple. In any event, the interview continued for an hour longer and not much business was discussed. At the end, Amy was pleased to offer her a job as Samantha was jumping with joy to accept it.

That night, the Duo appeared at the Dallas Grand Hotel. When escorted to the dining room, the Duo was shocked to not just find the 14 gals at their supper table, but the gals were surrounded by 20 men who all worked in their shop. So the Duo could only do what could be done. They ordered beer and wine all around, and joined the party.

*

Come Monday, the workers quickly settled in. It was Glen's decision to mix the teams with both men and women—and avoid an all- women's team. Each team had an experienced supervisor to include,

Paul, Vern, Finley, Elton, Elmer, and Glen. By the second day, the supervisor position was cancelled, and each man went back to fabricating casings.

Things were running smooth with Samantha and the fabricators when a surprise appeared in the waiting area. Sam saw the man, as he stepped forward, he hugged the man instead of just shaking hands with him. "Professor Winthrop, what a wonderful surprise. Let me fetch Amy out of her office." Amy walked out of the office as she spotted the professor. Amy did the same, but beyond the hug, she added, "welcome to our home!"

After all the greetings, Wendell finally admitted that he had several reasons for showing up unexpected. Included were, he'd always wanted to see the renowned place of two successful students, wanted to see if his women students had settled in, and was here to satisfy the request of someone above his pay grade. As the Duo started the tour in B-Wing, it became clear that Wendell did have an ulterior motive. The fabricating gals stopped their machines and came to greet Wendell with hugs and tears. There was plenty of soft private talk, but eventually Wendell freed himself and simply said, "thank you for taking care of my gals, they are all special individuals who dared to buck the old educational taboos. I'm beyond joy to see them well situated and so happy."

Resuming the tour, Wendell looked at the machine side. After careful consideration and measurements, Wendell asked, "can these machines be turned 90 degrees and be placed against the back wall in a straight line. "Yes, but for what purpose?" "For freeing up the front line where a third row of fabricating machines could be installed across the aisle—facing the first two brass fabricating machines." "I see, well let's finish the tour to see what else could be changed—but we can do it."

Once the tour entered A-Wing, Wendell kept looking at the old steel and storage room. Pulling out a measuring tape he said, "combining these two rooms would give you a generous space of 12 feet deep by 25 feet long. That means the partition wall would have to go as well as the two front walls." "Yes, that is possible." Moving on, Wendell saw the stacked crates of lead bullets at the end of A-Wing, but he didn't see any 231 grain 45ACP bullets and mentioned it. Those are in the warehouse where they were stored away till needed."

Walking in C-Wing, Wendell was impressed. Triple stacked crates of small/large primers, brass buds, and two types of powder—fast and slow burning. Wendell asked, "I noticed that you have two suppliers of powder, lead bullets, and brass buds. Why do you have only Winchester primers?" "Because we have a sound contractual agreement with Ira Winchester and he always keeps his word— we have an unlimited supply of these primers and at a discounted price to boot, for a regular monthly delivery of a 300-pound crate of 45ACP casings." "I see, very good. Now where are the 45ACP components?" "Right at the end of the warehouse."

Wendell was impressed at the amassed components for this new caliber. Across the aisle, Wendell noticed Walt at work refilling his tumblers. "What on earth is that man doing?" "He is processing 38 and 44 cases till they are cleaned and polished." Walt gave a demo. Sam then explained, "we decided that with this new caliber, we did not have the time to manufacture any other casing. So we bought 20 million 'once fired brass' casings at a very cheap price. Now we are cleaning them up and storing them. With a need of 10,000-20,000 cases a day, and a year with 250 workdays, we have enough casings to last 4-8 years or more of loading those calibers without resuming its case fabrication."

"Wow that frees your fabricators to concentrate all their efforts on making the 45ACP cases." "Yes, and that's the tour other than those processing tables you saw. So what are you up to professor?" "Can you trust me to pave the way and get your plant ready for a truly technical revolution that is possible in this building without a physical expansion. It requires some reorientation of space and ordering some parts." The Duo looked at each other and Amy said, "we're too young to not grow with the times, and of course we trust you professor."

With Sam's nod, Wendell said, "I need to have three things happen. First, have the carpenters pull out those walls and build a couple of bench tables with barstools, just like the loaders have, but without the backing. Then secondly, get your machinists to move those machines to the back wall. And third, ask your purchasing agent to order these brass pipes, steel parts, and small motors. You can get everything thru Big Blue in Arizona to simplify the order. The total cost will come up to $692.77 and it includes freight—or just order 'Package Winthrop,' heh?"

"How long to get this all done?" "We'll get Holiday Construction to do all the work, so my workers are not affected. They will have it done this week, I'm sure. We'll get Irene to order these parts and pay by telegraph voucher. When it gets here is unpredictable." "Yes, it is, Big Blue guaranteed the package would be on the train tomorrow morning and would be here in three days."

"Well, when can we plan on this revelation falling upon us?" "I will notify the powers in charge, and it can be any time after next Monday. I can only say that the item is coming from California and the people making this happen are also in California. I am certain that you will be very pleased with the entire project."

"Now aside from this project, let's talk about July 1st. I will have several six-month graduates in brass cartridge fabrication. I know you don't see the need for more workers now, but let's see how you feel after this project gets underway. It's been a nice visit, and we'll communicate again. You have a perfect plant and it's been a pleasure being here and seeing you two again. Before I leave, I want to visit with Neil, Elmer, Glen, and Irene—for old times' sake. Then I have to catch my train back to Houston. After a pleasant visit with all, Wendell took his leave with a tear and a smile on his face.

*

The week went by as smoothly as possible with carpenters being present all week. By Friday, the tooling machines had been moved, the old concrete holes plugged with fresh cement, and another six standard work benches made to match the row of six fabricating machines across the aisle. The new room made from the steel and storage rooms in A-Wing was done, and three more work benches built without backstop.

Curiosity was causing havoc amongst all the workers. When the Duo kept insisting that they had done the changes blindly at the professor's request, that they did not know the purpose, and that everyone would know its purpose as soon as they did—things finally settled down.

It was Monday morning and Ike had requested an emergency meeting with the Duo. As Ike stepped in the shop, the Duo was still busy opening the weekend mail, so he decided to walk around to see if anything was new. It didn't take a genius to see the physical changes but decided to not say a thing till the meeting was done. "So what's new Ike?" "Well you probably noticed that orders are low for all three calibers of 38 and 44 special as well as 45ACP. Whereas, orders are high for balance scales, priming systems, and powder measures."

"Yes, so what is going on?"

"Two things. The first is obvious. Smokeless powder is now commercially available, so gun shops are loading smokeless ammo and they all want the three new accessories—all as we had anticipated. Yet, there will always be a market for loaded 38 and 44 special ammo with smokeless powder—and that will be the plateau we anticipated."

"Now, something is happening with the 45ACP market that I had not anticipated. The big city gun shops have very large orders on the books, and will hold further orders till the pistols come out in May—which makes sense. The real surprise is what is happening in certain cities with a population of 5,000 and towns with populations of 2,500 to 5,000."

'Oh, please continue." "Let's take towns of 2,500 and up. These towns are surrounded by ranchers and farming homesteaders. The farmers don't have the income to get involved with a semi-automatic pistol since they still live by the double barrel shotgun for hunting and protection. Now the ranching cowboys took the last 20 years to get use to barbwire and fencing the ranches. They are not about to change their sidearms from the Colt

Peacemaker in 45 Long Colt to a modern looking and functioning handgun—that's a citified pistol."

Amy added, "wow, well that certainly explains what is happening to our orders. Thanks for all the 45ACP orders we got on file from your first pass to Texas gun shops. We'll probably be filling those right up to May." "Yes, but I suspect it will be weeks into June or July before new orders start coming back. So this is why I am here today." "Then go ahead, you have our attention."

"Well, I go back to your idea when we last met. I convinced you to put the Missouri marketing idea on hold. Now, I believe we have to jump in. Let me explain. Missouri has the same population as Texas, +-3M (million). Yet St. Louis has an incredible population of 600,000, which is the 4th largest city in the US. That is inconceivable, when you compare it with Denver 137,000 people, and Dallas's 42, 000 and our largest city of San Antonio at 53,000. Plus 250 miles west is Kansas City with its own population of 175,000 and also the 22nd largest city in the US. Heck it is 600 miles to St. Louis and 500 miles to Kansas City, compared to the 800 miles I traveled to Denver."

Amy added, "and with the estimate of 1,500 people per gun shop, that means 400-gun shops in St. Louis and 115-gun shops in Kansas City." "True, now the real surprise. I was at a shooting sports convention in Amarillo and was talking to a salesman from St. Louis. He said that ammo came directly from Winchester in New Haven. The problem was the ammo was slow coming in especially smokeless ammo. When I told him we were selling 38 and 44 special smokeless ammo, a progressive press that drops a loaded round with each pull of the handle, and prepaid orders for 45ACP; well the drooling was quite evident."

The Duo was pensive, but it was Amy who gave the first nod. Sam then said, "We see the business advantage, so how do you want to proceed?" "A bit different than I did in the past. Gun shop owners hate to hear a salesman's rhetoric, so it is harder to approach them with the verbal word, these owners are visual learners, and respond to the right visual stimulus. I plan to walk in, place three loaded rounds on the counter, wait a few seconds for the owner to realize what he is looking at and then add the lines; smokeless ammo as I point and say, 38 sp. 44 sp. and 45ACP. I again pause and finish, as I again point, with $3.50, $4.00 and $5.00—plus free shipping of $1.50 per 50-pound FR Box for your first unlimited order, as long as it is prepaid."

Amy said, "you are aware that you increased the 'special' ammo by 50 cents a box, heh?" "I know, I guess that's the price one pays to live in an out-of-reach area—you have to pay to play." Amy added, "and where did you get a rate of $1.50 for a FR50 box?" Those are Union Pacific rates in Missouri since they purchased the Missouri Pacific line some 10 years ago. One is only paying for the added miles and not for transfer to another line." Sam was listening when he threw a wrench in the mix. "What do you plan to do with our loading progressive press, do you walk in with your demo box or do you walk in just to sell ammo?"

"Oh boy, I did not anticipate that question. What it comes down to is that if I sell the loading press, then there will be less orders for loaded 38 and 44 ammo. I guess it's up to you, I'll do whatever you want." Sam answered, "right now, Neil has two workers, the experienced Titus and the new college graduate Stu. They are busy building scales and powder measures for our Texas gun shops who are now loading smokeless 38 and 44 special. But as you saw, we made some structural changes as requested by an advance man, Professor W. Winthrop. Now we are waiting for the project director to show up. That means that Neil's commitments, may change.

So since you are on vacation, if and when this surprise agent arrives, we'll send Cyrus to pick you up. Either way, before you leave on Monday, we'll have a definitive answer regarding the press's sale."

"So, much depends on this demo or this agent's plans." "Yes, and that includes my proposed market extension to Missouri, with either the promotion of ammo or our press, or both."

***

CHAPTER 10

The Automated Loader

It was a beautiful sunny January day in Dallas, with a mild temperature of 60 degrees, when two well-dressed dudes showed up unexpectedly at Cyrus's barn. Cyrus came out of the corral to greet the gentlemen when he found them inspecting the barn. The older gent asked, "are you the man who keeps this barn and the horses?" "Yes Sir, do you have a horse you need to be stabled or pastured for the day?" "No Sir, we are here on business and wanted to see what shape you maintained the horses, pasture, and barn. Do you have other duties other than this?" "Yes, I help the ladies unsaddle/ resaddle their horse, I run errands for Sam and Amy, I escort Amy or Irene on their telegraph runs, and I pick up items from the hardware store or pick up the biweekly payroll." "The payroll for

120 men biweekly has to be at least $5,000!" "No, closer to $6,000 in cash." "Hu-um, ever think of absconding with all that cash?" "Never, no worker would ever do that to Sam or Amy."

"How much are you paid for your work?" "I get the same as every other worker, $5 a day plus the 50 cent a day raise we all got at Xmas."

"That's a good salary!" "Yes, but we also get bonuses twice a year." "What, an extra week's pay?" "Oh no, several hundreds of dollars, plus many workers have started their own retirement account. Some of the gals have computed that these two bonuses last year came to +- $40,000 and it is called a profit-sharing plan." "Really!" Plus we have benefits: life insurance, short- and long-term disability, a retirement plan, a paid weeks' vacation, 3 personal days off, and several paid holidays."

"Wow, It appears this is a nice place to work and with such young bosses." "It is, and everyone feels the same. Whenever he asks for volunteers to work an extra shift, the entire group shows up—and it's not because of the time and a half pay. Our bosses protect their workers, and my new wife is proof of that." "I'm sure there is a story there, but I won't pry in your personal affairs."

"And by the way, I'm sorry for not introducing ourselves. My name is Ira Winchester, and this is my nephew Lionel Lofton." "Why of course, I hear your name on a regular basis. Pleased to meet you, my name is Cyrus Manning." The gents stepped up to shake Cyrus's hand. "Now, kindly send us to the shop's entrance." "Well, follow me, that is where I'm heading."

In the shop, Amy was busy with Samantha at the addressing table, while Sam was taking inventory with Irene in the warehouse. It was Hans who had just arrived who spotted the two strangers. Hans stepped up and took Ira in a powerful hug. "My goodness, Hans, what are you doing here, you sold this shop three years ago." "It's a fun place to be, and I guess I'm going to do just like you—die on the job, heh?" "Yes, we are old friend." After greeting Lionel, Hans went over to Amy. "Amy, we have special guests to see you." Amy turned around and nearly collapsed as she jumped for joy, for she was seeing a man who could only be a Winchester, as she also greeted Lionel, an old friend from the foundry. Amidst the commotion, Sam showed up with Irene. The smile on Sam's face said it all. Sam walked up to Ira and simply took him in a hug. "Welcome to our home, but I suspect this is not just a social visit."

"Well you know, old die-hard businessmen always mix socializing with a work- related event." "Ok, well let's have a cup of coffee in our office and visit a while." Irene was then introduced to the gents as they all moved to the office.

Lionel started, "we've been in San Francisco to look at what was advertised as a revolutionary machine." Ira added, "I traveled 3,000 miles, and picked up Lionel on the way. Lionel was the one who alerted me of this machine, since he had fabricated some new innovative parts for the inventor." "So, Professor Winthrop was doing advance work for you, I presume?" Yes, and if you are ready, I have a man waiting to bring in this machine which cost me $25,000 plus the $5,000 patent rights to use it, sell it, include it for a business deal, and duplicate it as often as needed."

"Great, let's do it." Lionel got up, and came back with parts of the machine. Setting up next to Neil's workbench, all the parts were then brought in. Ira then said, "this is Obadiah Greathouse, the inventor's nephew. He came with the deal. He will assemble it and give a demo. Meanwhile, Lionel quietly asked Luke to get some loading components for the new 45ACP—about a thousand of each component.

Curiosity was ruining the work cadence, and before everyone noticed, all the brass fabricators were watching Obadiah. Sam and Amy especially noticed how Glen was mesmerized as he saw the machine take shape. It was Glen who probably was the only one who recognized what this machine could do.

Ira finally added, "Like the semi-automatic pistol will shape the next 100 years, this machine will bring technology to an old manual process—and that is why you need to see it in action. When Obadiah was seen adding handfuls of casings, bullets, powder and primers, several faces started to change in early recognition. Then without any warning, Obadiah turned on the power and several motors activated. The carriage started moving, cases fell into place, then primers were added, followed by powder and bullets as the cases moved in a straight line from one station to another. When the first loaded round fell in the receptacle, and the next was only 3 seconds away, the spectators became bug-eyed.

The demo continued uninterrupted when the entire loading staff came to see the demo. The look on the loaders' faces expressed another silent feeling. It was Ann who said it best, "oh my, it may take some time, but this machine will be replacing us!"

Once everyone had seen the automated loader, Glen stepped up to examine the quality of the loaded ammo. It was Lionel who added, "Simon Granger asked me to make the many dies needed for automatic loading without manual involvement. They are different than the manual dies and we can make the twelve-piece die set for $58, as we guarantee them for 3 million rounds. I may add, this machine produces a finished round every 3 seconds, or 20 rounds per minute, or 1,200 rounds an hour, or 9,600 rounds per 8-hour shift, or 48,000 a week, or 2.5 million a year."

Sam was computing almost 10,000 extra loaded rounds per day with this automatic machine over the 90,000 rounds manually loaded each day by the workers. The daily fabricated casings came to 66,000, so 100,000 minus 66,000 equals a daily deficit of 34,000 cases. He extended his mental computation to the number of workers needed to load 10,000 and the answer quickly came to him— four manual workers to one man on the automated machine.

Glen finally had to ask. The machine cannot be left alone, so what does a workmen do all day?"

Obadiah answered, "he watches, anticipates an upcoming problem, handles the abrupt stoppages, lubricates the machine every two hours, adds primers, powder, bullets, casings, and keeps a foot on the dead man's pedal (the same kind of pedal on a locomotive that the engineer holds down and gets released if he suddenly dies). If he leaves and his foot comes off the machine, the machine stops. If he has to work on the machine as it is operating, he can deactivate the dead man's pedal."

With the demo hubbub having settled down, Ira asked that he, Obadiah, and Lionel meet with the Duo plus Neil and the man who could be placed in charge of this machine and other machines in the future. Sam looked at Elmer and asked him what he thought. "This technology belongs in a young man trained in machining, brass fabrication, and even manual loading. And there is only one man who fits that criteria. That's Glen, and I would rather stay with brass fabrication with my 10+ years left before retirement." Amy answered, "we agree 100%, but as family, we had to offer it to you first. You're a wise man father-in-law."

Once in the lunchroom with coffee all around, Ira started. "Now let's talk why we brought this machine to your attention. It is innovative and probably the machine that will commercialize the loading industry. It is very clear that this shop is planning for the introduction of the semi-automatic pistol and its caliber. There are no shops fabricating this casing or loading this round west of the Mississippi except for Arizona where Big Blue operates. California gets a share of that market, but we control the majority of the California market."

"So, it is up to you, Sam and Amy, to supply the major portion of gun shops out west—as a local producer, and let the big eastern factories supply the rest of the western states. To do this, you need to build your own automatic loader. You have the kit, and Obadiah will stay here for a week. He is a machinist, and if you add a few good machinists, he'll have it duplicated and running in less than a week. Neil perked up and said, "this is really important for this company. So, I will pull Glen, Elmer, Vern, Finley, Paul, Elton and add myself, Titus and Stu. With Obadiah's guidance, we'll have the machinists ready to build a second one when Obadiah is gone with your machine back to Connecticut."

Ira then addressed two more issues. The first, "I am giving you this $25,000 machine at no cost as long as you agree to increase my monthly allotment of 45ACP cases from 25,000 to 50,000 cases a month—at the same price of 11cents a piece. Plus we pay the shipping to Connecticut, and you maintain the 20% off on your unlimited primers— plus we sign a new contract, if you agree."

"To sweeten the deal, I jumped the gun. You know that it is not good business to fabricate those extra 34,000 casings at 'time and a half' every day. You need to add six more fabricating machines. So on our way back here, we stopped to see Big Blue. We do a lot of business with them and we got you a nice deal for six machines in 45ACP for the price of $22,000 instead of their usual $30,000. You can put two machines next to the backwall adjacent to the machining tools, and four out front. That way you save the space next to Neil to have two automated machines—one original to duplicate, and one being built. Besides, by July 1, Wendell and Elroy will have another fresh batch of brass fabricators—isn't it strange how things just simply seem to fall into place, heh?"

Lionel then added, "so you duplicate this machine, and when you're finished, you keep one here to use as your duplicating pattern. The other machine can be moved to A-Wing's space created out of the steel and storage rooms. And Glen can start loading while the machinists build the third machine. Oh, I almost forgot, Uncle Ira also gave you three of those 12-piece loading dies to get you started. So when you pay Big Blue for the fabricating machines, you'd better order two more automated loading kits if you want three active automated machines. By the way, we think that one man can only watch one machine with a dead man's pedal. In time, a man may be able to watch two machines with one pedal deactivated. I guess time will tell because right now it is still an unknown."

With the meeting coming to an end, Ira asked how things were going in selling 45ACP ammo. "Actually, things are slowing down and won't pick up till the new pistol is out, and then we expect a boom is sales." "So what are you planning to do till May, June, July or later—since the actual date is still not certain?" Sam knew that Ike was listening by the door to the lunchroom.

"We have a salesman that has covered Denver and several Colorado cities to the south, Plus Albuquerque and a few New Mexico cities. Of course, he has covered this state to the max. And now, we are planning to hit the next heavily populated areas to the north—that is St. Louis and Kansas City Missouri." "Excellent choices and not even as far as Denver. It is a shame that they are not getting a good service from the big northern industrial centers. You will have very receptive customers."

"By the way, how much are you charging for a 50-round box of 45ACP ammo?" "$5, and the customer pays shipping for a 50-pound fixed rate box that holds 15 boxes." "That's a good price for you, and a good deal for the customer. You'll get no complaints even if the gun shop tacks his 10% which comes to $5.50 a box. Heck some shops will add 15% to cover for shipping." "The nice thing about Missouri is that the Union Pacific goes to both these cities, so their FR box ships anywhere for $1 in Texas and 50 cents extra in Missouri— and that's a good deal."

Lionel then asked, if you cover St. Louis and Kansas City, but the 45ACP demand is still on hold, where do you go next?" "What we know we have is 600,000 people in St. Louis and 175,000 in Kansas City. Plus heading south from Kansas City we have Topeka KS with 34,000 people, Wichita KS with 25,000, Oklahoma City with 10,000 and Springfield MO with 23,000—for +- 90,000 people. We also have our progressive press for sale, but if Neil is busy building automated loaders, we'll have to put the press on the back burner."

Lionel added, "I see, well instead of doing a 'hop and skip' thru four cities between Topeka and Springfield, why not go north 175 miles to Omaha Nebraska with a population of 100,000 people— in one spot! Plus it's 650 miles back to Dallas compared to the 800 miles back from Denver."

"Hu-um, that is definitely worth considering."

Ira then added, "I see, I think I have a better solution after St. Louis and Kansas City. This is a new way to sell your product other than retailing it to gun shops. How about a large ammo distributor in California. Not individual gun shops, but a 'one site' to send your surplus ammunition. I am referring to a 'J D Watkins Inc.' in San Francisco. We are selling to him, but he always wants ten times more than we can send. It is 3,000 miles from Connecticut but only 1,500 miles from Dallas; besides J D pays the shipping anyways, and your $5 a box will bring a smile to his face." "Amy was quick to add, "that's a fantastic idea. Can you imagine all the paperwork and handling that would save. I like it and we'll send Ike or one of us to meet with him—that's the best idea of the day. Thank You!"

"On this line, when the demand goes out of control, it will be time for you to raise your prices. Anyways, you have a solid plant and solid plans, I wish you luck. Lionel adds, "get a local paper out of Phoenix to find out what's in the news, it might affect you."

The Duo then signed the new contract, as Ira and Lionel took their leave to the train depot. Obediah was already directing his team of local machinists to start building a duplicate automated loader. The plan was that as soon as the new machine was working well, and one man was trained in operating, maintaining, and trouble-shooting the machine, that Obediah would then pick up his machine and head to New Haven Connecticut to modernize Winchester's loading equipment. In this case, Glen would also have the benefit of the building experience, as it would help him to understand the intricate operational details.

*

When things settled down, Sam asked Cyrus to go to as many mercantiles as needed to find newspapers from Phoenix Arizona—even if it meant going to the city to find curbside newspaper stands. Then he and Amy were discussing whether to order six new machines and how many automated loader kits to order. Sam felt strongly that, at the cheap kit price of +- $700, they should add two more since the new workplace could handle a total of three machines on the backwall. Amy had no objections and pointed out that they would not replace loaders if they lost some workers. By following the rule of attrition, they would hopefully never have to lay off any loaders because of the three automated loaders—assuming it stayed at three machines."

When it got to discussing filling the last six spots in B-Wing with six more brass fabricating machines, it was Amy with the best argument. "It is always best to use present space, compared to expanding the building. Besides, it's a no brainer. We pay the worker $5.50 a day and he generates +- 1,000 45ACP cases a day worth 10 cents each, or $100. I'd say that is a good investment. Besides we need to stop 'time and a half' to maintain our minimum necessary production of new cases."

Sam came back, "in theory, this is all good financial planning, as long as we can find trained workers to operate the extra fabricating machines." "True, but I suspect that Professor Winthrop has that covered, don't you think?" "Ok, and we'll work on this problem of "time and a half' tonight after supper." That afternoon, Irene was at the telegraph office to order two more "Winthrop kits" and six fabricating machines in 45ACP.

Meanwhile, Ike came back after his late lunch to get his marching orders. "Well Ike you saw the demo and overheard the business meeting. So what do you think?" "Well to me, the primary reason to go north and take on new customers, is to guarantee there does not persist the 45ACP lull we are now experiencing, especially if the pistol is not released in May." "True, the question is whether we also push the 38 and 44 special smokeless ammo as well." "And whether we try to peddle some presses for either BP or smokeless ammo—and only add the scale, priming system, and powder measure if they sign the liability waver if they still insist on using the powder measure with BP."

It was Ike who spoke first, "well, it's your decision, but this is a 'one time' visit to +- 500 gun shops, and I personally think I should mention all three items, when pushing the prepayment of the 45ACP loaded cartridge." Sam looked at Amy and added, "he's right, let's present all three products. Neil just pointed out that it would probably take a month to get all three automated loaders built, but afterwards, he, Titus, and Stu would then be free to build press accessory parts. So, let's go over the prices. A box of 38s at $3.50, 44s at $4, 45ACP at $5, the press now at $60, the accessory kit at $15, the scale at $10, the priming system at $20, and the powder measure at $25. Stop at the post office and verify the price for an out of state 50-pound fixed rate box to either St. Louis or Kansas City." "And I assume we still place 24 ammo boxes of 38's, 16 boxes of 44's, 15 boxes of 45ACP in a 50-pound FR box?" "Yes, plus the press also fits in a special FR-50 box as the scale, priming system, powder measure, and the accessory kit fit in another FR-50 box." "Ok, I'll be leaving in two days, and you should start getting orders soon. Once I have the money in hand, I'll telegraph you with the order as I place the funds in a Wells Fargo bank for automatic transfer to your town's Wells Fargo as we've been doing." "yes, and good luck as you stay safe, heh?"

*

That evening, while preparing supper, Amy was peeling potatoes at the sink when Sam came to her, started kissing her neck, then pulled a HIP as Amy responded by turning and kissing him. Before they realized what was happening, they found themselves copulating while standing at the kitchen sink. Afterwards Amy asked, "what brought that on, not that I objected!" "I was watching your back and behind, and I could not resist making love to my old high school classmate and friend." "Well, that was certainly a memorable event, but if you ended up impregnating me, we'd have to call our child with a name tied to the kitchen sink, heh?" "Oh well, there is nothing wrong with 'Pealer' or 'Scrubber,' heh?"

After supper, the Duo knew they had an issue to discuss and come to a mutual business decision. While Amy was doing the dishes, Sam picked up the two newspapers from Phoenix that Cyrus had found. As Sam was scanning and reading titles, looking for something that could apply to their business, a title caught his interest— "College graduates seeking employment in a saturated market, and college officials are to blame."

Sam started reading as he caught Amy's attention, "Amy, listen to this article out of Phoenix."

"The Phoenix College of Trades announced that 20 brass cartridge fabricator Xmas graduates were looking for work in a saturated market. All factories using fabricators in Arizona, Nevada and California were 100% staffed, and no spots were available for recent graduates. These young men and women will have to seek employment out of state and region. Allegedly, the college officials knew the market was saturated and should have either informed the students, or close the department till job markets opened up. If anyone knows of a factory that has openings, please send telegram to Jarod Bloomfield, the group's representative, at 14 Waters Ave, Phoenix AZ."

By the time Sam finished reading the article, Amy was in the kitchen's door and said, "that sounds like what Lionel was referring to. With Big Blue showing up anytime, and the two colleges in Texas won't have any graduates till June 1st, I think we should send Mister Bloomfield a telegram that sells our shop—and remember that the article mentioned that these students were both men and women."

Once settled in the parlor, the Duo tackled a tough issue. Sam started, "we are definitely heading for 18 brass machines. So, let's theoretically present what 18 machines can produce each day." "That's easy—5,500 X 18 = 99,000 new casings each day. But that won't start till June unless we can hire some available workers from Phoenix." "Don't we have a surplus of 45ACP casings on reserve?" "No, we did but they are now gone." "So we are at the mercy of our loading staff, and with Ike on the warpath, we'll soon be in trouble."

Sam pondered the situation and finally said, "I've been avoiding this solution for years, but I now believe it is necessary. It is time to start a second shift five days a week and avoid weekend work. I propose that each day, between 5PM and Midnight, that we have a 'voluntary' work shift at full standard wages. The benefit will be a 7-hour shift with a half hour late supper or snack break at 8PM. If you think about it, at a full staff on 18 machines, that means 90 fabricators. I'm sure we'll get each worker to at least work one extra second shift a week—and likely these young new workers will be glad to make the extra money. With trained workers, they don't need five men to run a machine—the worker can do all five jobs and produce the average of 1,100 cases per shift." "I agree with you, the time has come. Plus, if we produce a surplus, we can sell them to Ira and make some good money at 11 cents a case."

The next day, Sam placed a telegram to Arizona.

To: Jarod Bloomfield
14 Waters Ave
Phoenix, Arizona

From: TEXAS LOAD
C/O Sam Balinger
Industrial Park, Dallas Texas

AWARE OF SITUATION STOP

HAVE FABRICATING SHOP WITH 60 WORKERS STOP

HAVE 30 SPOTS AVAILABLE STOP

SHOP AT +- 115 WORKERS, 40% ARE WOMEN STOP

OFFERING $5.50 A DAY AND BENEFIT PACKAGE STOP

SEND A SCOUTING PARTY OF 4 PEOPLE, WILL PAY FOR TRAIN TICKETS, HOUSING, AND MEALS.

ENCLOSED IS $50 VOUCHER TO EASE TRAVEL STOP

IF ACCEPT, COME DURING WEEK TO SEE SHOP IN FULL OPERATION— STOP SAM

By the time Sam got to work, the machinists were busy studying plans, diagrams, and measurements. Then Obadiah assigned each one apiece to make. It was a slow process, but Obadiah insisted on not cutting corners. He knew that for this machine to run as flawlessly as possible, that every part had to be exact duplicates. Sam figured he had enough things to do, so he stepped away as Big Blue arrived with six crates and went to work.

During the morning's first break, Sam addressed the workers in B-Wing. The announcement that every evening would have a voluntary second shift with a clarification of benefits was well received especially by the young workers. For security reasons, at Midnight the security company would provide a large wagon to bus the workers back home.

By 5PM, Sam appeared at the B-Wing to see how many workers would stay for the second shift. Thirty-nine were staying, and Sam gave them all a choice to work with a full team, a partial team, or even to work solo if they preferred. Sam wrote down the worker's names for the payroll ledger, and left for the night. It wouldn't be till the next morning that Kent reported, 40,000 casings by weight, had been fabricated by the second shift.

That same morning, the telegraph messenger arrived with an emergency telegram. Sam started to read:

SCOUTING PARTY ARRIVING TOMORROW STOP

LOOKING FORWARD TO TOURING YOUR SHOP STOP

THANK YOU FOR THE $ ADVANCE STOP

ETA 9AM, WOULD APPRECIATE PICKUP STOP

Well Amy, it looks like we'll be entertaining a scouting party tomorrow. Let's prepare by reserving two rooms in the Dallas General and we'll help out in the shop today while we still can. Who knows how the next few days will go."

*

At 8:30AM, the Duo was on the platform. The train was on schedule and the Duo had held breakfast till the scouting party arrived. When the whistle sounded, the Duo never realized that a surprise was at their waiting. Waiting for the passengers to disembark, it was Amy who spotted two hand holding couples looking about the platform for someone to greet them. As the Duo stepped up, they asked, "are you the official scouting party for TEXAS LOAD?" "Yes, we are looking for an older gentlemen by the name of Sam Balinger." "I am that man and this is my wife Amy, we are the owners of TEXAS LOAD." "Oh my, we didn't know!" "Like we didn't know you were obviously two committed couples." "Is it a problem that we are not married, and that half of our group in Arizona is half men and women." "Absolutely not, welcome to Dallas. Have you had breakfast?" "No, and we are starved. I have to admit that we ran out of money after supper last night."

Walking in Darcy's, the Duo ordered for everyone, steak, eggs, bacon, pancakes, toast with preserves and peanut spread, and plenty of coffee. The young couples were busy eating and not a word was said till after their stomachs were filled. Finishing their coffee with toast and that new peanut spread with raspberry preserves was a delight for all.

Finally Jarod said, "this is my special person, Adelle Crenshaw, and these two are Marc Sims and Susan Sotherby. We have been training in brass fabrication with minors in machining and metallurgy for the past six months. We are all very capable of fabricating any pistol or rifle caliber. We especially like 45ACP because it is so short and easily draws into a case, plus it has the rebated rim with the undercut extraction groove." "We see you are happy to be here, but how do you feel about moving here permanently?" Jarod added, "Adelle and I are ready to build a life in a new state if that's where fate takes us. And I may add that the sixteen fabricators we left in Phoenix feel like we do. Besides leaving 100+ degrees in the summer would be a blessing." "Then, let's go to our shop and see what you think."

Riding to the shop, the Duo gave their guests a quick tour of the suburb that they lived in with all the services available without going into the city. Arriving at the Industrial Center, the four visitors realized that this was a clean industrial area. Seeing the tri-wing building marked with the TEXAS LOAD sign, the visitors knew they arrived at their destination. Entering the complex, the group looked a bit surprised, and it was clear that they never expected to see what was in front of them.

The tour started at the office, down to the lunchroom, to the unoccupied room, and finally to the loading section. Sam started, "we have 36 loaders who put out 90,000 loaded rounds a day, and these processing tables box and ship all these rounds every day. The 90,000 rounds are all new 45ACP brass that our B-Wing fabricates each day." Walking into the warehouse, it was clear that they had massive surpluses of loading components and millions of brass buds.

Amy finally said, "and now to B-Wing which is what you came to see. We encourage you all to ask questions of any worker and then we'll visit in the office. Standing in the archway, Sam took over. "On the left is the original fabrication center of 12 five-man machines. At the rear is the steel storage room and the processing center for the presses we sell to gun shops—yes, the same machines you saw our loaders use. On the right are our dozen machining tools and the last six fabricating machines being installed by Big Blue, that actually need 30 new fabricators—yes, that is waiting for you all."

"Now, this strange machine that is being duplicated is what will be moved to the empty spot you saw in A-Wing. Obadiah will start the machine to show you what it does." As the machine started spitting out a fully loaded round every 3 seconds, the look on the four faces would never be properly described in the written or spoken word. Finally, it was Marc who said, "I had heard about these machines but never thought I would ever see one. Now you tell me that you plan to keep duplicating them and have three of them. I am very much impressed."

Amy then added, "go ahead and mingle and ask anything you want to know," as she instructed the twelve machines to take a break and answer the four guests truthfully. The Duo gave their guests a half hour to rove around and ask rather poignant questions. Amy heard things like: "What's it like working for young bosses?"

"Is the pay there on pay day or is it delayed?"

"Are benefits followed to the written word?"

"Any bonuses ever given?"

"Do you ever regret leaving home and moving to Dallas."

"If you could do it again, would you take a job here?"

"Are women respected for their work?"

"Do women get equal pay than men?"

"Do men resent women making the same salary?"

"Are you happy in Dallas and in this shop?"

Sam had been talking to Obadiah when he came over to Amy. "So what kind of questions are they asking?" "Well I just heard Susan ask if you had a habit of 'hitting' on the women workers—being so young and all!" "Oh, does that mean that I should be doing that—like a herd bull doing his job?" Amy didn't even hesitate, she put her hand around his neck and let him know that this specimen was all he needed to service. Of course Adelle and Susan saw that display of emotion. After the break was over, the guests were asked to meet in the office.

The Duo then pretended to check things with their workers to let their guests speak amongst themselves. As the Duo walked in, they were asked what the beginning salary was, and what benefits were provided to new workers. Sam was short and sweet as he said, "As college trained people, your pay starts at the top rate of $5.50 a day, with full benefits of ....and the recent added option of working a second shift five days a week from 5PM to Midnight, with an armed bus service to your home after Midnight. Any other questions?"

The two couples looked at each other and Jarod was given three strong positive nods. "We are drooling at the possibility of joining your company and these mixed workers. How do we apply, and if accepted, can we start working tomorrow?" "Whoa, we accept you and to be truthful, we need you more than you need us. So, go back to Phoenix and please convince your sixteen classmates to join you."

Well Mister and Missus Balinger, we came to visit and to stay if you accepted us. We have all we each own in two luggage. As we are broke, we would be willing to start work tomorrow." "No, here is $100 for each of you, a joining bonus, you have three days in a hotel with meals to find an apartment, buy an upgrade in clothes, minus the free uniforms in the water closets, and other necessary personal items you need. That will bring you to Monday when you can start work as your machines will be installed by the Big Blue technician. Also, please ask your sixteen classmates to join you. We will start looking for boarding houses or apartments for couples before they arrive. Here is $175 in cash to give to the telegrapher to give your classmates for train tickets to get here. You can also tell them that a 'joining bonus' awaits them upon their arrival." Adelle added, "there are 8 men and 8 women, all single and unattached. They are all very capable fabricators, and you won't be disappointed."

Over the next week, these four college graduates were certified as capable of working independently. In due time, the remainder of the class would arrive and would be set to work at a total of four machines. By the end of 10 days Ike's orders were arriving. It was clear that most of the orders were for all four products. At the same time, the first automated loader was moved to the prepared room in A-Wing and Glen started producing 45ACP loaded rounds.

***

CHAPTER 11

Tweaking for the Future

Within three days, the last 16 fabricators arrived. They were broke but that was overshadowed by the eight gorgeous lady fabricators they included as classmates. After receiving the usual $100 sign on bonus, the college graduates were farmed out to their boarding houses. When they arrived at the shop, they were all given their shop uniform and put to work. The Big Blue technician had three machines completed, so five guys helped him put the fourth machine together so they could get to work. The technician would then finish the last two machines by himself.

Elmer or one of the old essential workers supervised them for a half day, and then let them loose to work independently. Sam had been praised for hiring trained workers with a young and new twist to their methods. By the end of 10 days, the last two machines were installed but left without any operators. So, until June 1st, the fabricators would number 80 fabricators once the three automated loaders were built and the older fabricators would be back to work—minus Glen who would run the new automated loaders.

Once two of the automated loaders were operational, Glen called Sam over. "It is now clear to me that I can watch and service two machines but three is too much. Besides this new space is not working out since we can only put three machines per row, which means that the next three machines will be in the front row. One man cannot watch two machines in two different rows." Sam appreciated the situation and finally said, "the future is clear to me, one day we'll likely load only with the automated machine. So, right from the start, you need to start your own row in the A-Wing. Let's call Ann over and reorganize."

The result was that Glen took over row #1 and moved six of the most independent loaders to the new room. The remaining 30 loaders lost one of their loaders. Craig Dufield, Ann's assistant, would be moving over to Glen's row and be responsible for machine #3 and #4. Ann would need to find a replacement assistant before she moved six operators to the new room. Craig would start a training program immediately. To make this happen, Irene was sent to the telegraph office to order Kit #4 ASAP. So the attrition program had now started with the manual loaders—the first down and many more to go.

While the boys were moving, Sam started to take an inventory of supplies. Once he became overwhelmed with the count, he decided to wait for Irene to return. Irene laughed as she added, "actually, I guarantee you that we have enough brass buds and loading components to produce 100,000 pieces a day for six months. This surplus will get rotated once a year. So what I'm doing every day is replacing the components and brass buds needed to load 100,000 rounds a day. Now that is a feat in itself." "How is that, Irene?"

"Well, let's take the 230 grain bullets. There are 30 bullets to a pound and that converts to 9,000 bullets per 300-pound crate. Now, since we load +- 100,000 rounds a day, that means eleven 300-pound crates. The same holds true with brass buds, it so happens that there are 18,750 buds in a 300-pound crate. Or, that's another 5 crates for Kent to move each day, and that doesn't include the primers and powder. Once all these 15 crates are pulled out of the boxcars, he then has to expedite them to the loaders and fabricators. Meanwhile, Luke has to expedite the remainder of the components, move addressed boxes to the loading area and a whole bunch of other duties." "Hu-um, what are you driving at, Irene?" "Sam, we have gotten to over 120 workers, and 10 more coming in June, and we now have a second shift of fabricators to supply. I really think those two expediters need some help." "Clearly, that was well said, and I'll take care of it. That's why you're in a position to see the need. So, Thank You."

It was a week later, when things were running smoothly, that an interesting subject came up. Someone mentioned that it was time to practice shooting if one wanted to join the local speed shooting club this spring. The subject kept going from one person to another when Elmer suggested that the shop should have its own team and compete against the local teams in each of the three big Dallas shooting clubs. It was Amy who asked how many people were interested and had a Model 1898 New Service DA revolver in 38 special with two speed-loaders. Hands went up as Sam wrote down the names: Sam, Amy, Glen, Irene, Elmer, Luke, Neil, Ann, Jarod, Adelle, Marc, Susan.

Sam was impressed, especially at Luke who had apparently been practicing with Elmer. "Ok, we can have a team of 12 people, and call ourselves TEXAS LOAD SHOOTISTS." Sam then added, "that name allows us to add new members without changing the name. In order to train and prepare those representing our shop, we will practice every Tuesday and Friday night, and shoot any Sunday when they start competition shoots in May till the fall. As shop representative, you get 100 free rounds for each practice and for the Sunday shoot. Anyone who wants to add a Saturday practice before competition gets another 100 free rounds. If you miss a practice, you still get the 100 free rounds. We'll try this for the summer to see how it goes. Do you all agree?" It was a unanimous yes.

The practices started immediately and quickly became a social event. Lucille and Ida came with Luke and Elmer, and had as much fun as the shooters. Of course, this early in the practice season, several blunders were seen to everyone's amusement. The common ones were: releasing the six rounds from the speed-loaders onto the ground instead of the cylinder, fumbling the speed-loader reload, forgetting how to walk fast between targets without tripping, missing easy targets, shooting the wrong targets called for, and silently swearing at that rotating five target nightmare—now being called the Texas Star, and a few other chosen names. After the practice came out the thermoses full of coffee and the many pastries as a snack. The practices lasted between 6:30 to 8PM and all 100 rounds had been sent downrange courtesy of TEXAS LOAD.

Over the weeks, many of the new fabricators and some old loaders showed up at the practices. Some with co-workers and some alone to watch the shooting. It was Sam who saw future shooting members as Amy saw future weddings.

The mid-week and the end of week practices were a welcomed recreational event after busy days at work. Finally April arrived, and with an early spring, the match director, Winston Hutchins, arranged for a competition between the TEXAS LOAD SHOOTISTS and the local club's best dozen shooters—now called the DALLAS MARAUDERS.

The week of the competition was a serious time during the evening practices, and everyone showed up for a Saturday practice. Plus, Sam had brought an extra 1,000 rounds and the team managed to eat those up as well. By Saturday night, the team was ready and eager to compete.

Competition day was a busy time at the range. Shooters were charged a $2 registration a piece plus another $3 for a third speed-loader and its belt holder. Amy smiled as she paid with a company voucher and handed all the shooters their third speed-loaders— so each time on the shooting line would take 24 rounds to complete the sequence. Spectators were welcomed free of charge, as most of the bleachers were full of TEXAS LOAD workers. By the time shooting started, it was standing room only.

When the shooting was about to start Sam walked right into Ike. "What are you doing here, you're supposed to be in St. Louis?" "I've been there three weeks, and this is my week home. We'll have our business meeting tomorrow, but today it's competition. I was a member of the DALLAS MARAUDERS long before I joined you and Amy. So, today I have to maintain my roots—so good luck!"

Before the shooting started, the Match Director explained the targets and how it was scored. "The total time for a shooter is the time it takes to shoot all four 6-shot arrays. All missed targets are a 5 second penalty added to the shooter's time. The first six shots are on six falling plates, and the plates have to fall, not just turn or move. The second row of targets are the shooting tree where all right-hand green targets have to flip to the left and show red. The third set is the pendulum where six discs are swinging like the pendulum of a clock. A hit will knock the disc off. The last six shots are on the dreaded Texas Star where a plate knocked off will start the wheel to turn to compensate for the new weight distribution. If all five plates are knocked off, a rather small center fixed plate of 3 inches across is the final shot. If hit, it will be a bonus of 5 seconds off his score compared to a 5 second penalty if missed."

Once the shooting started, the shop workers were amazed at the coordination and skill their team was demonstrating. Several members were keeping score of every shooter's time. The funny stage was the Texas Star. It was clear that the spinning wheel could take hold and drive the shooter berserk. Fortunately, it was the last array and would not ruin the result of his first three arrays, but would hurt his standing.

For weeks of practices, since the practices were on the actual targets that were used during competition, Amy had kept score of everyone's times and the changes over the weeks. Sam's total time to run the arrays and shoot 24 rounds was broken down as: shoot falling plates (6 seconds), reload (3), and walk to next array (4) for a total of 13 seconds. Similar time for the shooting tree and pendulum for a subtotal of 39 seconds, and the Texas Star for 7 more seconds—for a grand total of 46 seconds minus 5 seconds for hitting the 3-inch target in the Texas Star's center. So a very good time was 41 seconds with no misses or fumbles. Looking at the ledger's record, the slowest time was 52 seconds where the average was 46 seconds—a rather respectable time distribution for competition.

The shop team had understood the dynamics of the Texas Star—hit the top plate, then right to left quickly, and right to left again quickly. This did not throw the weight distribution off much as long as you did not linger between the right and left shot. Then the 3-inch center target did take a second extra to get the sights tight on the target.

The real show was the Marauders. It was clear that they needed to better understand the physics of the Texas Star. It was funny to see some shooters mess up. One gent shot two right target in a row and the wheel went amok as the shooter emptied his gun and missed every plate. Another shot the right target but missed the left one and the spinning started. The solution to a spin was to wait till the wheel came to a stop and restart. Otherwise, shooting at a spinning wheel would guarantee a miss on every shot. One shooter was so disgusted that he promised the match director that he would return after dark and spot weld the plates to the frame. One shooter told the match director that this was an impossible target to hit. So the match director looked at the now still Star, took his chewing gum out of his mouth, threw it at a plate and planted it dead center as he said, "it's easy if you wait till it stops spinning," as the crowd fell apart with whistles and guffaws.

The competition allowed all 24 shooters to shoot the array twice and the best time was counted for score. Sam had his best score of 45 seconds to match Ike's 45 seconds. The TEXAS LOAD SHOOTISTS won the days competition by a mere 20 seconds of total time. For the top gun, a special shoot-off was scheduled—a Texas Star shoot-off. Two right plates would be yanked off by a rope behind the shooter. The wheel would go wild, and the shooters would have to decide whether to wait till it stopped spinning or shoot on the fly and risk several 5 second penalties.

Ike lost the draw and had to go first. He decided to wait till the wheel settled down with the remaining three targets at 3-6-9. He then shot the 3 and then the 9 plates and the single 6 last for a total time of 17 seconds. Sam decided to start shooting when the spinning stopped, and the remaining plates started to swing as on a pendulum. Then he would shoot at a plate when the plate reached its apogee. He repeated the same on the other two targets and his total time was 14 seconds. His shop fans started to hoot and holler as they celebrated their team's success.

All in all, it was a memorable day for everyone. And everyone suspected that the team size would soon increase in numbers. Ike came over to congratulate Sam as he added, "I couldn't lose to any better man!"

*

The next morning, Jarod came to see Sam. "After yesterday's competition, I have a dozen men and women who want to buy the gun kit from the Whitehouse gun shop, and want to start training to become the second shop team. Mister Whitehouse was at the shoot and was advertising his speed shooting kit to include: the New Service Colt

Model 1898 pistol in 38 special for $30, a gun belt and holster for $5, three speed-loaders with three holsters for $10, which included a pouch for empties and used speed-loaders. The package came to $45 per kit and the 12 candidates have $450 to make the deposit so Mister Whitehouse can place the order."

Sam thought, "are they serious to do this?" "Oh, yes. These guys and gals have worked since high school just to pay for college. They have never had a hobby nor were they ever interested in one until yesterday. The only issue to clarify is whether you will honor their goal by allowing the same free ammo you offered your team?" "That offer is good for anyone who want to compete and represent the shop. But, on second thought, wait her, I'll be right back." Sam walked into his office, and came out with a paper that he gave Jarod. "But Sir, that's a bank draft for $300!" "I feel good about anyone in this shop who wants to join the rest of us gun lovers. Besides the free ammo, I'll give them one full Saturday afternoon to train them with the rules and safety of the sport. Then a team captain will need to be elected to be in charge of the team. I have enough of managing my own team, heh?"

That same day, Ike arrived for an important meeting. "Well, things are certainly different in Missouri compared to Colorado, New Mexico and Texas. This 'show me, I'm from Missouri' motto is changing the entire retail market. First of all, half of the gun shops do not believe that Colt will actually come out with a semi-automatic pistol in a new caliber. So these gun shop owners are not interested in preordering a 'ghost' ammo in 45ACP. These gun shops have just begun selling VP certified pistols for smokeless powder—and these are mostly the old-style Colt Peacemaker."

"So are they ordering our 38 and 44 ammo, and what do they think of our reloading press?" "Yes, and the orders will reflect this. Now the reloading press is an interesting issue. When I walk into a Missouri gun shop, the workers yell to the owner, "out of state 'drummer' at the counter." That brings out the owner, but when I place my box on the counter and open the side door, all eyebrows point to the ceiling. The rest is history. In the past 2 weeks, I visited six gun shops a day for 10 days and I sold 30 presses with scales, priming systems, powder measures, and accessory kits. Plus all the 38 and 44 ammo—prepaid ammo and press."

Amy added, "I certainly agree with you, the orders reflect it. Now what about the gun shops that believe the Colt pistol is soon to come out?" "They are thrilled to see a drummer, and they even know of TEXAS LOAD quality ammo. These shops are ordering anywhere from two to five 300-pound crates at 90 fifty round boxes per crate or 4,500 total loaded rounds per crate. The price per crate is $495 plus shipping at the present rate of $5.50 per 50 round box. It is also interesting that these shops are not interested in the loading press. They are only interested in selling the finished product, which is also why they are ordering crates of 38 and 44s."

"So, assuming the type of gun shop runs 50/50, we can almost expect an average of 15 press orders per week." Ike came back, "yes, and that means that Neil may run a back log, so I'll start preparing a numbered list as who is next to get their press delivery." Sam finished the meeting by saying, "so far we can handle the present orders, so we'll see how things progress as we meet again after two weeks of work in Missouri."

*

The next weeks rolled into months. The first thing that people knew, it was April 1st. Despite Ike gathering orders at a steady rate, the shop was finally building two surpluses. The fabricators with their second shift finally had a surplus of 45ACP casings. The loaders were still putting out 90,000 rounds a day, plus Glen and Craig, were now putting out 40,000 rounds a day. This finally led to a surplus of loaded 45ACP ammo—loaded with a 230-grain bullet and 6.0 grains of medium rate burning powder. When the Duo asked Irene to go over the exact surplus count, they were shocked.

Irene started, "as you can see, we have 15 crates of 45ACP casings ahead, and each crate has 25,000 casings worth $2,500. Plus Elmer and the four essential workers are now back at fabricating cartridges now that four automated machines are in full operation." Amy did some ciphering and said, "that's $37,500 sitting in the warehouse—not good for cash flow!" Sam then said, "send 6 crates to Winchester each month till we are down to a surplus of 4 crates, and then try to keep it there. But most important, watch this surplus carefully, since it is the base for our present production."

"Now, what does the loaded 45ACP ammo surplus look like?" "We have twenty-five 300-pound crates in the warehouse—that's 2,250 ammo boxes or 112,500 rounds, and we are adding 5 new crates each day." "And that pattern will continue till the new pistol is released. Those 25 crates are worth $13,500 if sold at $6 per 50 round ammo box."

Amy summarized, "So, every week we are adding another 25 crates of surplus loaded 45ACP ammo—or another $13,500 in limbo. So where can we find a buyer for 50 crates of loaded ammo worth $27,000." Sam was thinking as he added, "and likely will continue all April if Colt releases it May 1st. But what if they don't release it till June 1st?" "Then we'll have 100 extra crates for April and 100 extra crates for May in surplus—which ciphers to $13,500 X 8 = $108,000." "No way, we have to find someone to buy 50 crates, and more if necessary."

The Duo was pensive as Irene softly added, "I think Ira Winchester said it best—J D Watkins, Inc. out of San Francisco California—the statewide distributor of 'guns and ammo' for 1.5 million people. The alternatives are Chicago Illinois 1,000 miles or Seattle Washington 2,000 miles. To me, the best choice is J D Watkins, who has dealings with Ira Winchester. As you recall Ira's words how Missouri was not well treated by the Illinois distributor, and Seattle is just too far. Sam looked at Amy and said, "San Francisco is 1,500 miles or +- 37 hours of traveling time on a train—are you game?" "Sounds like good talking material in our parlor tonight, heh?" "For sure!"

*

After supper, the Duo had to make a decision. Amy started saying, "there is no doubt, we have to meet Mister Watkins to set up a working relationship. Afterwards, it will all be telegraph communications, bank transfer of funds, and freight by train. What we don't want is to sign any contract that promises the delivery of mandatory minimum amounts on a regular basis—only Ira gets that type of arrangement. What he gets is our surplus, and if there is no surplus, then there are no deliveries."

"Gee Amy, you sound like you're giving me your business thoughts. Are you not coming with me?" Amy stopped in her tracks as she got up to get her large business bag. She pulls out a bag of soda crackers and sits down to speak. "You see dear, I missed my monthly four weeks ago and now I'm again late. Yesterday I had morning sickness till about noon. So, I think I'm pregnant."

Sam had an enlightenment, he looked at Amy and saw her guardian angel smiling and holding a baby wrapped in a blue blanket. He then got up and sat next to her on the settee. He took her in his arms, kissed her gently, and said, "you have been a total woman and wife to me. I will spend the rest of my life committing myself to you—I love you so!"

"Now let's get real, have you seen Doc Kipp yet?" "No, it is way too soon. From what I know, the first 12 weeks of pregnancy determine if the pregnancy will continue or miscarry. I am at most only 8 weeks along. Yet, 40 hours being rocked on a train, and the rocking aggravating my morning sickness is not something to look forward to. Plus, were I to miscarry, then we would always blame the train trip as the cause, even if unlikely. Plus, getting medical attention on a train or a small town is also not the wisest of choices were I to miscarry. So, I need to stay home and continue working in the shop."

"You lay a strong argument; except I don't want you to stay home alone." "Ok, I can always go to mom and dad's house, or even Glen and Irene's house." "Plus, take it easy and let Samantha lead the process of filling orders. And don't forget, you have our son to feed and grow." "And how do you know it is a son?" "Oh, a beautiful angel told me so!"

*

Sam packed a carpetbag of personals and change of clothes. He was wearing his New Service pistol and brought a book on managing employees and controlling the growth of a successful company. Once getting his tickets, he bought passage on a luxury train that was an express passenger line. So, he paid for the extra Pullman sleeping berth and three meals a day in the dining car.

To pass the time, he read, napped, visited with other passengers, and managed not to get bored. In reality, it was a real rest from the daily routine at the shop. It was a fine day when suddenly the trains rocking and clickety clack went silent, when a man stood up with a gun in hand and yelled, "this is a hold up, and you have 10 minutes to put your cash in this bag before the next watering station." The conductor then stepped into the passenger car and froze in place.

Sam again realized that he somehow attracted this kind of activity. After noticing how nervous the robber was, he decided to disarm him instead of killing him. Sam stepped right up to the man and said, "you don't want to do this, give me your gun or I will have to draw my gun and shoot you dead. As an alternative, if you abandon this robbery, I will solve your problems that led to this unfortunate decision to become an outlaw." The would be outlaw caved in, and holstered his gun. "Great, now I'll end up in jail with a wife and three kids at home without income."

"Sit down son, why did things get this bad for you to consider this?" "I was laid-off six weeks ago in San Antonio, and have not found a replacement job. Actually, with a shop going bankrupt, the town was flooded with unemployed workers who ended up taking all the menial jobs." "What did you do for work and where did you work?" "I was a foreman machinist in a large factory by the name of Holt Industries." "Did you say Holt Industries?" Yes, Winston Holt was the owner."

"How much do you owe?" "Two months' rent and credit at a mercantile for a total of $129." "Are you and your family willing to move to Dallas?" "For gainful employment? Absolutely." "What is your name?" "Cletus Moore."

Sam looked at the conductor and asked, "are you willing to give this man a second chance; if you are, I'll transform his life forever." "Sure, why not!" "Well Cletus, you and your family are in luck. I own a shop in the Dallas Industrial Park called TEXAS LOAD. Give this note to Neil, and he'll get you started making small parts. When you get a chance, see a worker called, Glen. You might have a surprise. To make this happen, here is $300 in cash. Pay off your bills, move your family, get a clothing upgrade, but not the shirt, the shop has its own free shirts with a logo. Get off at the next town and go back to San Antonio to make this all happen."

The remainder of the trip was uneventful. He finally arrived in San Francisco at 1PM. He took a taxi to JD Watkins workplace and went straight to his office. "Hello Ma'am, my name is Sam Balinger, and I would like to see Mister Watkins." "Oh, so you're the man referred to my husband by Ira Winchester. We sent you a telegram yesterday, only to get an answer from your wife that you were already in route. Sorry we missed you, we could have avoided that long 1500 miles by train. Anyways, you are here, and JD is waiting for you."

"Hello Mister Watkins." "Please call me JD if I can call you Sam?" "Of course!" "The reason I tried to contact you is because I need a beginning supply of 45ACP loaded ammo before the pistol is released soon. Right now, I don't have a single round, and my customers are screaming at me; and accusing me of poor planning practices. I begged Ira Winchester to send me at least 500 ammo boxes to at least give my customers two 50-round boxes as absolute minimum. His answer was that he had zero supply to send me. That is when he told me to notify you. And here we are. What is your actual business and what do you have for sale?"

"I have a shop of 140 workers. We fabricate brass cartridges, load them, and sell them to gun shops over four states—Texas, Colorado, New Mexico, and now Missouri. We actually have been fabricating and loading only 45ACP since January1st, and we can now load 130,000 rounds a day between manual and automated loaders. Which is why we now have an excessive surplus that is tying up our cash flow."

"Well, that can be good news for us, do you have a sample of your load?" Sam hands JD a full box. JD takes out his calipers and starts taking several measurements. JD finally says, "nice case, all measurements to trade standards, nice rebated rim with TEXAS LOAD stamp, nice undercut extraction groove. Taper crim to specs, I presume? What is the load?" "Medium burning rate powder loaded to 6 grains to generate 850fps with a 230 grain RN hardcast lead bullet."

"Perfect, all set to acceptable shooting specs by Colt. Nice job. Before we talk money, let me tell you some secrets. We are only 75 miles to Santa Cruz where California Powder Works has their plant. Their fast- burning powder will finally have a name –Bullseye. Plus I hear that Dupont's medium burning powder will be called Unique. Within a few years, we'll have several new powders with a commercial name and a place on the burning chart from fast to very slow." "Interesting!

"The other news, "once this standard load is out, the speed shooters will then change the load to a 200 grain RN bullet behind 4.5-5 grains of Bullseye, with the recoil spring changed from 16 to 14 pounds. The change in recoil spring will be a 'drop in' type and no other changes will be needed to get it to properly cycle and eject spent cartridges. Just keep this in mind and follow your local speed shooting clubs." "Also interesting and likely important to know."

"Now, let's talk how many crates you have for sale and how much do you want for each box of 50 loaded rounds." "I have a surplus of 50 crates......"

"WHAT, I couldn't get Ira to send me 5 crates and

you have 50 crates for sale. Are you for real?"
"Oh yes, but this is a one-time sale, and not tied
to any future contract. I can say, that if the Colt
pistol is not released till June 1ˢᵗ, that I'll likely
have another 50 crates for sale." "Oh my, well how
much do you want per 50 round box?" 50 cents a
box more than what I get in Texas because someone
on the train told me that the gun shops planned to
retail a box for $7—if they could get some for sale."
"Well you know that everything in Texas is bigger,
but everything in California is more expensive—
and that's the way it is. So, again what is your final
charge for a single box."

"Fifty 300-pound crates come to 4,500 fifty
round ammo boxes. At $6 a box, that comes to
$27,000 and you pay for your own shipping. Unless
I am mistaken, you'll be able to supply your 250
customers over 100 ammo boxes each. With the
balance spread out, it will keep them satisfied until
you get resupplied by another manufacturer. Once
the pistol comes out, I suspect you won't be getting
any deliveries from us."

"We have a deal, let's go to the Wells Fargo
bank and make the deposit as a bank transfer
telegraphically to your bank in Dallas." "Actually,

this is going to our account in the Wells Fargo Denver branch."

*

Sam's return trip was uneventful. He returned to Dallas at 6PM and went straight home as he had notified Amy of his scheduled return. After the usual intimate greeting, Amy handed Sam a telegram she had received today from Ira. Sam started to read:

OFFICIAL—COLT PISTOL TO BE RELEASED MAY 1ST --STOP

ONLY SEND WIN THE AGREED 2 CRATES/MONTH --STOP

SEND NO MORE AMMO TO JD WATKINS --STOP

TIME TO HOARD AND BUILD SURPLUSES --STOP

IN POSITION TO CONTROL PRICES IN YOUR 4 AREA --STOP

RETAIL AMMO PRICES FOR PISTOL EXPECTED TO SKYROCKET OUT OF CONTROL --STOP

A REASONABLE PRICE PER BOX WILL GUARANTEE YOU THE EXTENSIVE MARKET FOR YEARS TO COME--STOP

PRICE GOUGHING HAS NO LONGEVITY IN THE BUSINESS WORLD--STOP GOOD LUCK--STOP IRA WINCHESTER

Sam looked at Amy and said, "that changes everything." Amy interjected, "our loaders, fabricators, and the automated machines are running at full operations. We are building surpluses and filling all our orders. What can we do different this early in the game?" "Being on trains for days, I've had time to think about this. Ike is home this week, let's send Cyrus to pick him up; then we need an emergency meeting with the six foremen." "Uh-uh, since Glen moved to the automated machine, we don't officially have a foreman in brass fabrication." "Correct, let's solve this immediately." Sam walks to B-Wing and says, "we need a foreman for this 80-man section. I present five candidates: Elmer, Vern, Finley, Paul, and Elton—the original five fabricators before I even bought this shop. You have a half hour to put your written choice in this box. Plus I want an assistant foreman to be in charge of the second shift at a foreman's full pay. Anyone of you five want that job?" Elton's hand went up. "Yes, my wife was switched to the second shift at the sewing factory. She likes it, so I'd like to try it as well." "Done, so you have to choose between these four men. Start voting."

While the voting was going on, Neil came to see Sam. "Cletus is a major addition. He is a very capable machinist and he'll be useful with all those press orders. So, thanks!" "Has he made contact with Glen yet?" "Oh yes, a very emotional meeting, but I know nothing about it, heh?" "We'll I'm sure there is a story there, and we'll eventually hear the details."

With the voting done, Luke and Irene were tabulating the votes. Irene showed Sam the results. "With a vote of 72 in favor, Elmer is your new foreman. Elmer, will you and Elton join us for an emergency meeting, and congratulations on the high vote—a vote of confidence."

The meeting started as Amy read Ira's telegram. Sam then took over. "We are now in a major race to build as many surpluses of 45ACP casings and loaded ammo. Amy, do we have any unassigned backup workers since our last round of training loaders?" "No, one lady floats between my table and Ida's processing table. One man has become the third expediter, and the last three are now full-time loaders. The foremen have their teams working at maximum efficiency, so any changes have to come from you, Ike, or the foremen. Otherwise, the next three weeks will be full steam ahead."

Sam was bold to ask, "does anyone have any ideas what we need to do either differently or add new strategies." There was total silence in the lunchroom, so Sam finally spoke up. "I want us to put out a huge mailing to every gun shop in the four-state area. We have the addresses for Texas, Colorado, and New Mexico, as Ike has St. Louis and Kansas City. Prepare several flyers. One to remind everyone that a proposed Colt pistol release is likely going to be May 1st and suggest how gun shops should be preparing for the new pistol. A second to provide a current order form with a current price list. It should include a notice that the 45ACP price per box is going up to $6 effective June 1st."

"The third flyer is because of the successful purchase of 38 and 44 special 'once fired brass.'"

I propose we alert our gun shops that we will take our own TEXAS LOAD casings back and pay ¾ of a penny each."

Eyebrows went up as Elmer asked, "is this financially worthwhile compared to the cost our shop can produce casings?" "Yes, I've checked the statistics. Our cost to produce one finished 45ACP casing is 1.5 cents. That is based on fabrication expenses: 5-man day labor of $27.50, brass buds for 5,500 cases of $55, and processing agents of $2.50 comes to a total cost of $85 plus cost of electricity. If we can purchase them at ¾ of a penny, we can have Walt process them, and then we can load them. In return, the newly fabricated 45ACP casings can be sold to Winchester for 11cents a casing—minus a penny for the brass bud. I'd say that is good business. Besides, it will probably take a month before we start receiving 'once fired brass' with our TEXAS LOAD stamp."

Amy saw positive nods everywhere. "Does anyone have anything to add?" With no comments, she added, "nice job Sam, I guess Luke, Ike, and me had better get to work on the typewriter and printing press, heh?" As Luke adds, "and send

Cyrus to get a large bottle of ink, 3,000 sheets of paper, 1,000 envelopes and 1,000 2-cent stamps."

*

It took a week for all three well written flyers to be mailed—and it included all 1,000 of them. For the next three weeks, the workers were working well as the fabricators were filling the second shift with about 80% of the daily staff. It was at that time that the Duo met with Ann.

"I'm sure you're aware that the second shift is very popular, and we wondered if it would be possible to have a daily second shift with our loading staff. This would be a voluntary participation and can be as little as one evening or all 5 evenings a week. Amy and I are expecting an unrealistic demand for loaded ammo to feed this new semi-automatic pistol. Being three weeks to May 1st would be the perfect time to get a second shift started if possible." Ann was very interested and said, "I will present the idea tonight and ask everyone to come to work tomorrow prepared to vote yes or no by private ballot like you just did with the fabricators—everyone thought that individual secret votes was a nice touch to add."

The next morning, the Duo heard Ann, "Time to vote. If you are willing to work at least one evening shift a week then vote yes. Otherwise it is a no vote." The vote was interrupted by Ray Perkins, Ann's new assistant foreman. "If there is a second shift, I would be willing to work it as the shift manager five evenings a week." "Excellent, let's vote. The total votes included 36 manual loaders plus Ann, Glen, Ray, and Craig's vote. Tabulation by Luke showed a vote of 32 in favor. Ray would change from days to evenings as a regular worker, and Ann had to choose another day assistant. It was Sam that said, "second shift starts tomorrow night for the next month—on a trial basis."

*

May 1st arrived, and the Colt pistol was released throughout the US, including all points west of the Mississippi. For two weeks, nothing happened except the pistol's popularity was mentioned in all circles. The on May 20th, the post office delivered 30 envelopes. Each one came from one of the four states, and it was for a crate of loaded 45ACP ammo for each gun shops—per flyer notice. A 300-pound crate held 90 ammo boxes at $6 each, and all orders included a telegraph voucher for $540 plus $5 for shipping. Fortunately, 300-pound crates had been prepared in advance, and stored in the warehouse without an address till the orders would come in. Now it was just a matter of adding the address, an invoice, and load it in the freight boxcar.

Madness reigned for the next months as the loading and fabricating second shifts were continued with good attendance. The days rolled by and the orders were still coming-in out of control. As the end of June arrived, it was time for the six-month meeting to be held the Friday before the July vacation—and before the last 10 college fabricators arrived.

That day, no one worked. Payday was held that morning for the past two weeks, and of course the weeks' vacation pay was added—so for three weeks the pay at $5.50 a day X 15 days was $82.50. Some of the workers had second shift pay, during those two work weeks, added that also ran anywhere from 1 day to 10 days. Then, the social hour with beer, wine, cheese & crackers, and other unmentionables prepared by Darcy's Diner, was a huge success. The hot meal of chicken and dumplings or shepherd's pie was well received. After the classic dessert of Apple pie a la mode with coffee, it was time for the business meeting.

Sam got up and started. "Looking around, many of you look tired and I hope you rest up and enjoy yourselves this week, for you have earned it. Now you know the supply still cannot keep up with the demand that this popular pistol is causing. So, we have decided to make an offer to everyone. If any of you decide to work any one day or more during your vacation, either day or evening shift, we will pay you time and a half." The place erupted in laughs, guffaws, whistles, and applause. Sam came back, "this is 100% voluntary, and it is our attempt to avoid the usual backlog of orders that a closed shop always yields."

After the crowd settled down, Amy then took over. "This season, everyone was so busy, that we did not do the individual assessments for the bonuses. We are now 140 employee strong, soon to be 150, and we gave you $28,000 in profit sharing. That comes to $200 per worker." Again the place erupted. The Duo started passing out the envelopes containing two $100 bills in US Currency. It was clear that the young workers had never expected this kind of bonus after only six months on the job. As people started to leave, Cletus came to the Duo and handed his envelope back to them. "I've only been working here a month, glad to be here, but I cannot accept this money." Sam took the money and put it in Cletus's shirt pocket, "Neil is very pleased to have you aboard, and your family needs this buffer. So take it, and we'll hear no more of it, heh?"

*

During the vacation, the Duo was at the shop each day. The first two days were skimpy, but by Wednesday the day shift filled up, and by Thursday both the day and evening shifts were well attended in all departments. By Friday night, the shop was in a good shape with all orders caught up and surpluses were even added to. Amy was showing fatigue and Sam took over her job and had Cyrus bring her home after dinner. Although she did not yet show that she was in the family way, everyone in the shop knew she was on her way to motherhood.

The next thing to happen that week was the arrival of the last 10 college boys and gals—7 men and 3 gals. Their arrangements had all been completed so their settling in was as smooth as possible. Elmer and the three essential workers supervised them for a day, then left them to their work—the advantage of hiring college trained machinists.

It was mid-July when Winston Hutchins showed up at the shop.

. "Hello Sam, we've missed you at the range, especially with the new Colt pistol the club is training with." "I know, but this is a madhouse here with the demand for ammo, so we and all the workers have to rest on Sundays. Eventually, we'll all get back into the game with the new pistol. So what brings you here today?" "The standard powder load of 6 grains of this powder now called Unique, over a 230-grain bullet, simply beats the shooter and with the excessive muzzle jump, it actually prolongs his shooting times. The speed shooting standards are changing and wondered if we could order a couple 300-pound crates of....."

"I know what you want. You want 200 grain RN bullets over 5 grains of Bullseye powder with a reduced recoil spring of 14 pounds instead of 16 pounds. The resultant velocity is still 850fps but with less felt recoil and less muzzle jump." "Exactly, and if it works out, the other two speed shooting clubs in town will follow suit." "Sure we can, hold on," as he waves Irene over. "Irene, how long to get some hardcast lead 200 grain RN bullets sized .451, here for a special order?" "Uh-uh, well, you see, we have ten 300-pound crates in the warehouse. Each crate has 10,500 rounds or the number to make 210 ammo boxes per crate!"

"Really, and whose idea was that?" "Lionel Lofton, when he was here with Ira! He said to order ten crates and some day you would be happy they were already in the warehouse." "You see Winston, with the right staff, I don't need to think anymore. We'll have those ammo boxes for you in a few days." As everyone started laughing.

The steady orders were helped along by Ike pounding the streets in St. Louis. He was now getting a full crate order at each gun shop. Some even tried to pay for two crates which Ike refused. He explained, "my bosses prefer to send 90 ammo boxes (one 300-pound crate) to any and all gun shops. When the 90 ammo boxes are sold off, you are free to place another order by telegraph with its voucher included. Ike reminded every gun shop owner that TEXAS LOAD does not fill orders on credit. Payment must be included by slow post office private bank draft or fast telegraph voucher. The telegraph system was considered an absolutely secure method of payment, whereas the post office mailbag was often robbed out of stagecoaches and even the railroad express car.

Along with selling the ammo, he continued to sell the reloading press. The real surprise is when he convinced gun shops to start returning 45ACP "once fired brass" for a credit. The returns were plentiful, and as soon as Walt cleaned and polished them, the workers started reloading them as the newly fabricated casings were accumulating as a surplus for later use or for sale to Winchester.

In short, the Duo realized that the business had been tweaked to its maximum, and every day was now a glide thru the week. That evening, the Duo was in a reflective mood. Amy pointed out that orders were plentiful, the fabricators were at maximum production, and the loaders who had loaded new casings were now reloading "once fired brass." She finished her thoughts by saying, "things are good the way they are, we did well to get the business to this point, but where do we go from here?"

Sam thought, "well for the foreseeable future, I suspect things will stay the same. However, eventually things will change. I include:

1. One day all of A-Wing will be the site of a dozen automated loading machines. It will be a case where four automated machine operators will each supervise three machines and those four men will replace the 36 manual loaders we now have.

2. One day the west will have three major ammunition distributors. Watkins will do the west coast, we will control the central Midwest from Texas to N. Dakota, and Chicago will do the eastern portion of the Midwest. Winchester and other big eastern manufacturers will supply Watkins and Chicago, and we'll supply the remainder.

3. One day, I'll probably collaborate with Glen and we'll build a real progressive press for individual hobby use. Lionel will build the frame, and Neil will build the accessory parts. This machine will add bullets and cases automatically, and every time you pull the handle, a finished round will fall in the box—with the operator's other hand tied behind his back."

Amy suddenly jumped in, "Ok—STOP! I can see your brain never turns off. For now we have a great business, so let's enjoy it the way it is." "Ok, but let's not forget where we come from!"

"Oh, the memory is stored forever—we started as classmates and buddies. After high school, I became a court stenographer as you went to work with Sil and Wil as railroad marshals. When we found each other, we became partners and I bought us a business out of your nest egg. Then the best part occurred, WE FELL IN LOVE and married. The story continued with us going to college and you designing a loading press, started loading ammo from the fabricated brass cartridges your machinists produced, and the business grew from then on. Today, three years later, we have more money in the bank than we'll ever need, have sellable business assets of a quarter million, and support 150 employees."

Sam smiled and added, "Yet, the most important thing is that we proved that FRIENDS COULD BECOME LOVERS, and together could build a future for themselves!" "True, but who would have thought that it would be a business making brass cartridges and loading them to live ammunition, heh?" "For sure!"

***

The End

AUTHOR'S PUBLICATIONS

Non fiction

The Hobby/Cowboy Action Shooting.................. 2010
44Magnum/Shooting a Classic Big Bore.............. 2016
RELOADING/A Practical Hobby..................... 2017

Fiction in modern times

Cowboy Shooting/On the Road................... 2018
Cowboy Games........................... 2018

Western fiction (circa 1880-1900)

Wayne's Calling/A Paladin..................... 2018
Sylvia's Dream/Olericulture.................... 2019
Cal's Mission/Victim's Justice................. 2019
Paladin Duos............................ 2019
US Marshal: Jake Harrison.........(pandemic)... 2020

Printed in the United States
by Baker & Taylor Publisher Services